———————— ★ ————————

In the distance, we could hear the faint sound of a siren. "I think she had a heart attack. I don't believe we could've saved her."

Amelia Lever had been a large unattractive woman with bristly gray hair and a prominent nose. Her dark purple lipstick made a garish contrast to her white face. There was a flesh-colored patch on her upper arm. A nicotine patch? Could you wear those and still smoke?

"Was Mrs. Lever trying to quit smoking?" I asked.

The principal pointed to the pile of cigarette butts sticking in the trash can filled with sand. "I don't think so. Miss Jacey said she lit up before she was out the door. She smoked for about three minutes and then got kind of glassy-eyed and said her heart was racing."

"That looks like a nicotine patch on her arm," I pointed out.

"Could she have overdosed on nicotine?" the other teacher asked. "That's possible, isn't it?"

———————— ★ ————————

A LITTLE LEARNING

JANE TESH

W🌐RLDWIDE®

TORONTO • NEW YORK • LONDON
AMSTERDAM • PARIS • SYDNEY • HAMBURG
STOCKHOLM • ATHENS • TOKYO • MILAN
MADRID • WARSAW • BUDAPEST • AUCKLAND

To all my friends at Jones School,
dedicated, talented teachers who truly made a difference
in the lives of their students

Recycling programs
for this product may
not exist in your area.

A LITTLE LEARNING

A Worldwide Mystery/July 2012

First published by Poisoned Pen Press

ISBN-13: 978-0-373-26806-1

Copyright © 2009 by Jane Tesh

Printed in U.S.A.

Acknowledgments

I would like to thank Dr. Jennifer Chapman and pharmacist Tim Matthews for their helpful information and Sharon Lowe for her legal advice.

A little learning is a dangerous thing.
　　—Alexander Pope
　　　　　An Essay on Criticism

The one parts with its life there,
And the other loses her soul.
　　—Jacques Offenbach
　　　　　The Tales of Hoffmann

ONE

I'VE OFTEN SAID I don't want to have children, and now I know why. I already have three. This bright Sunday morning in September, I came downstairs to find three heads bent over a patchwork of brightly colored cards spread across the kitchen table. The black hair braided with yellow beads belonged to Denisha Simpson, age ten. The green and purple hair sticking up like wiry weeds was attached to her best friend, Austin Terrell, also ten. The light brown hair that could benefit from a good combing belonged to my best friend and new husband, Jerry Fairweather, who is thirty going on ten.

"Okay, we've got all the Pond Palace series except the Drawbridge of Death and the Dungeon of Despair," Denisha said.

Austin moved one stack of cards to another. "Here's all Bufo's Webbed Foot Guard except for Rayford the Sticky-Tongued and Bart the Beeper."

"Weapons over here," Jerry said. "Sword of Destruction, Sword of Light, three Sword of Revenge cards. Can we trade one? What does Ronald have, Austin?"

"I asked him. He won't trade."

"Sword of Justice, Sword of Peace. We're missing the Sword of Illusion."

"That's really hard to find."

I went to the coffee maker. "Good morning, Warrior Toads."

Three heads came up. Three voices said, "'Justice Rules the Swamp!'"

"So I've heard," I said. "How's the collection coming along?"

"We need about twenty-five more to complete the first set," Jerry said.

"First set?"

"Set two comes out this week and set three in December just in time for Christmas."

"Someone is a marketing genius."

Austin rearranged the cards. "We weren't doing too well on our own, but when we combined our sets, we had almost all of them."

"And Jerry bought some more," Denisha said.

I pushed back my tangle of dark curls and poured a cup of coffee. It was typical of Jerry to spend his money on Bufo the Warrior Toad cards instead of buying normal things or paying outstanding bills, but I really couldn't complain. Being married to him is everything I hoped it would be: intensely satisfying, especially in the bedroom, without sacrificing the fun we've always had together. And he was actually working. Before we'd got married, Jerry and I made a bargain that if I'd go back to my artwork, he'd give up his scams and get a legitimate job. To my surprise, Jerry had found a job at the local bookstore and enjoyed it.

"Can we go to Georgia's today and get a few more packs?" Austin asked him.

"Sure. I'll be working there today."

I leaned against the counter and sipped my coffee. As for my part of the bargain, well, I hadn't been as successful. The portrait of children I painted for the local theater had brought me a few more commissions, but I wasn't painting as much as I should. I kept telling myself my detective work kept me busy, but that was stretching the truth.

You can't fuss at Jerry for stretching the truth, now, can you? I told myself, and a little worrisome thought wormed its way into my mind. I looked at my slim, youthful husband, his gray eyes shining as he and Austin argued the merits of Bufo's Glowing Sword versus Bufo's Wart of Power. I'd known Jerry since we met in college, and he'd been very good at keeping his schemes and his problems secret from me. But I recognized the signs. Something was going on, but I couldn't tell what.

He looked up and smiled that smile that had won my heart from the first time I met him. "What's up with you today, Mac?"

"I thought I'd go in to my office for a while."

"Meet you for lunch?"

"Shana wants me to meet a friend of hers. I'm hoping this will lead to another case."

I tried to put my worries aside and concentrate on my new career. My fledgling detective agency could use all cases possible. I'd known when I moved to Celosia the small town wouldn't have much use for a private investigator, but I'd already solved two murders.

"It's been almost two months and no one's felt the urge to kill," Jerry said. "Either you're slipping or Celosia is."

"People are beginning to eye me strangely. I thought about putting the Grim Reaper on my business cards."

"What do you want for breakfast? The kids and I had cheese toast."

"That would be fine."

I took my coffee to the front porch and looked out across the fields surrounding the Eberlin house, the house Jerry had inherited from his uncle. We were still in the process of remodeling. Goldenrod and white Queen Anne's lace shimmered in the morning heat. In the oak trees, cicadas whirred like tiny buzz saws. Beyond the dusty driveway and wandering rail fence, the highway led about a mile into town where Georgia would be opening her bookstore and maybe a few minor crimes would occur. Some shoplifting, perhaps, or a serious case of littering. Something calm and normal. I really didn't want to get involved with another murder.

After a while, Jerry came out with my cheese toast on a plate. "Breakfast is served."

"Curb service. How nice." I sat down in one of the rocking chairs.

Jerry perched on the porch rail and admired the view. He had on his khaki slacks, white shirt, and a yellow tie decorated with flying pigs. "And it's going to be another hot day."

I set my coffee cup beside my chair. "I hope Nell's coming to install the new air conditioner."

"She said she'd get to it today."

The ancient upstairs unit had finally died. Fans helped a little, but in our part of North Carolina, the heat can continue long into October. "Great," I said. The cheese toast was a perfect combination of crunchy toast and gooey cheese. "This is great, too. Have you ever thought about being a chef?"

"One career at a time, please."

I licked an extra bit of cheese off my finger. It had taken a lot of wheeling and dealing to get Jerry to find any sort of job. I wasn't going to push. "How are things at the bookstore?"

"I'm helping Georgia rearrange the magazines. She wants to put in a line of greeting cards."

He continued to look at the fields, but I could tell his gaze was miles beyond the trees and wildflowers. I never dreamed he would ever settle down, much less with me in an old house in a small town, so I wondered if he missed his wandering life. I was glad Austin's and Denisha's Bufo obsession was keeping him occupied.

He brought his calm gray gaze back to me. "Ready for seconds?"

What a loaded question. "With the kids here?"

He grinned. "They need to go get more Bufo cards."

"What were you thinking about just then?"

"Besides you?"

"Not getting restless, are you?"

"No."

"Not feeling the urge to sell fake pocketbooks or play mind reader?"

"Just let me hold an occasional séance and I'll be fine." He put his arms around me. "Actually, just let me hold you."

We were enjoying a long soulful kiss when behind us we heard Austin say, "Eeeuww."

Denisha said, "Austin Terrell, that's perfectly all right now that they're married. You ought to watch and see how it's done."

"There's no way I'm kissing you!"

Denisha was unfazed. "One day you will."

Jerry gave me another quick kiss before letting go. "Come on, kids. We'll ride into town with Mac and see what's at the store."

WE HAVE JUST one car, my light blue Mazda, so, after dropping Jerry, Austin, and Denisha at Georgia's Books, I went to my office. My office is located in the Arrow Insurance building, just down the hall from Ted Stacy, a tall, dark Southern gentleman, who was one of my first friends in Celosia. The letters on my door still say, "Madeline Maclin Investigations." I'd wanted to add "Fairweather," but Jerry convinced me that would be too long. Jerry and I had spent most of Saturday in Parkland visiting his brother, so I hadn't had a chance to check my messages and look through my mail. Besides the usual bills and flyers, there was a card from my ex-husband, Bill, announcing the birth of his third child. I sat looking at the card for a long time. Hooray for you, Bill. He'd always wanted children, the main reason our marriage fell apart. Never mind that Bill was also domineering and thoughtless. I'd never felt any maternal stirrings, and to him, this made me less of a woman. Between Bill and my mother, who tried her best to make me into Miss America, it's a wonder I have any sense.

Well, now Bill had babies and I had my own career so we were both happy. I had to chuckle as I read the new baby's name. Darlan Kyle. Boy, girl, or alien?

The next piece of mail was a letter from a friend in Richmond, congratulating me on my agency. Thank you very much. I took a moment to look around the room. I had a small oak desk, bookshelves, filing cabinet, a beige and green armchair for my clients, and a view of trees and the swing set in the next yard. Pleasant and useful, a direct contrast to the hot dusty office I had with an agency in Parkland. There, I had been one of many investigators hoping for a scrap of a case.

Here, I was my own boss, and even if I didn't have a lot of work, at least I was in charge.

The third letter was from the Weyland Gallery, one of the many art galleries in Parkland. I frowned as I opened the letter. I didn't know anyone at the Weyland Gallery. I'd like to know someone at the Weyland Gallery, because it's one of the most prestigious in the city. I wondered how I'd gotten on their mailing list. My frown turned to open-mouthed astonishment as I read the letter. I'd been invited to enter the New Artists Show.

"Dear Ms. Maclin," the letter read. "We are pleased to inform you that your application for our New Artists Show has been favorably reviewed, and we invite you to enter three pieces of your choice. Please bring your work to the Weyland Gallery on Monday, September 23. The show will be on Saturday, September 28, at 8:00 PM, followed by a champagne reception. We look forward to presenting your work to our patrons and sponsors."

The letter was signed, "Letticia Booth, curator."

I read the letter again. I looked at the envelope. Was this a joke? Application? Favorably reviewed? I hadn't sent anything in to any gallery! How had I managed to get into a show in Parkland? Who in the world knew that I even painted—

Jerry.

I knew something was up! Oh, my lord, I was going to wring his neck! I was punching the bookstore phone number furiously into my phone and growling about the various means of strangulation when I stopped. A man stood in my doorway, one hand raised as if to knock.

"I can come back," he said.

I felt the heat rise to my face. "No, please come in. Sorry about that. A little burst of temper. Nothing serious."

The man looked about thirty years old. He had reddish hair and little round glasses. In his neat buttoned-down shirt and sharply creased slacks, he reminded me of one of my history professors. He smiled. "A dissatisfied customer?"

"No, no. Just a little family matter. I apologize." I held out my hand. "I'm Madeline Maclin."

He shook my hand. "Nathan Fenton. I was hoping to find you in today."

"Please have a seat, Mr. Fenton. What can I do for you?"

He sat down in the chair opposite my desk. "Well, here's my problem. I've received a very curious gift from my late uncle, and I'm hoping you can help me figure it out." He took a piece of paper from his pocket and slid it across the desk to me. "I've inherited some money from my uncle, but I can't get it unless I solve what appears to be a riddle of some kind."

The flowing script was easy to read. "To my nephew, Nathan Ellis Fenton, I leave a fine fortune, provided he unlocks this puzzle and finds the one true key." The next part made little sense. "'From west to east the river flows, from ancient times the sparrow flies. Trust animals that live in packs, and listen where the portrait lies.'" I looked up. "Do you know what any of it means?"

"There's a river nearby, but it doesn't flow west to east."

"What about the portrait? Have you looked behind all the pictures in your uncle's house?"

"That's another problem," Nathan Fenton said. "He moved out of his house. He lived in a trailer. He didn't take any portraits with him. I'm at a loss."

"And the sparrow? Did he have a bird?"

"No pets. He hated animals, so the trust animals line doesn't make any sense."

"The poem must mean something else," I said. "What else can you tell me about your uncle? When did he pass away?"

"Last week. He was seventy-five and had been in poor health for years." Nathan Fenton sighed. "He wasn't the friendliest man in the world, but he loved games and puzzles. I'm really not surprised he would leave a riddle. The trouble is, he probably sent this riddle to other people. It would be just like him to have folks competing for the same prize."

"Was there a will of any kind?"

"Yes, he left the family home to my cousin's wife, Victoria Satterfield, as well as enough money to maintain it. Apparently, this riddle is his idea of a treasure hunt."

"Any idea how much money is involved?"

"Elijah did well on the stock market and owned quite a bit of land that he sold. I imagine the prize is several hundred thousand dollars, maybe even a million."

"Who else is likely to be included in the hunt?"

"I have the one cousin, Aaron Satterfield, but Elijah could've sent the riddle to anyone."

"Does your cousin live here?"

"No, he's in Parkland."

"Give me a few days. I'll see what I can do."

Fenton looked relieved. "I don't want you to think I'm anxious about the money, but I have a chance to buy a camp about ten miles from here in Westberry. I don't know if you've heard of Camp Lakenwood?"

Being in Little Miss pageants gave me no time to enjoy summer camp. "No."

Nathan's eyes gleamed. "It used to be a wonderful camp. I went there every summer. I learned to fish and row a canoe and build a campfire. But the owner can't keep it up and wants to sell it. It's my dream to fix it up and have a camp, not only for the kids who can afford it, but have it free for underprivileged children."

"That sounds wonderful."

"But according to Misty May, my uncle's lawyer, I have to solve this riddle by Monday, September 23, or the money goes to—well, I honestly can't believe this, but she says it's true—a fund to build bat houses."

"Bat houses?" Jerry's Uncle Val had studied bats. I thought we were through with them. "You mean the little wooden shelters to put on trees?"

"Yes. Isn't that the craziest thing you ever heard of? And he hated animals! It's some kind of stupid joke."

When Jerry and I moved to Celosia, we thought it was pretty small, but since then, we'd learned that the town had a population of over eight thousand—ten thousand, if you included some of the little adjoining neighborhoods. And yet there were two batty uncles in the neighborhood.

"Did your uncle know Val Eberlin? This sounds like one of his projects."

"I don't know where Elijah got the idea. Probably to drive us all bats."

"Is Ms. May in Celosia? I'd like to speak to her."

"She has an office in Rossboro." He dug in his pocket for his cell phone. "I have her number."

Nathan Fenton had to solve the riddle by September 23, the day I was supposed to have three pieces ready for the Weyland Gallery. That gave me a week. I hesitated just a moment and decided if I wanted to paint and detect, here was a chance to see if I could do both.

Nathan gave me the lawyer's number. "I don't have Aaron's, but he's in the phone book."

"I'll get right on it."

After discussing my fee, Nathan Fenton wrote me a check, shook my hand, and left. Since this was Sunday, I didn't expect either Misty May or Aaron Satterfield to be at work, so I left messages on their answering machines, asking them to call me. I read the poem again. Well, you have a case that doesn't involve murder, I told myself. Solving cryptic riddles may not be your idea of fun, but you need the work. Besides, something like this will keep Jerry occupied for hours.

Which reminded me.

I called the bookstore and asked to speak to Jerry. He sounded extremely innocent.

"Yes?"

"There was a certain letter in the mail today from the Weyland Gallery."

"Was there?"

"It seems I'm invited to enter three pieces in their New Artists Show."

"That's great news."

"I'm wondering how I managed to enter a show without knowing about it."

"The world is full of unexplained phenomena."

"Jerry."

My tone of voice must have warned him not to go any further along the psychic highway. He began to laugh. "Congratulations!"

"Jerry, how did you do it?"

"I know people."

"In the art world?"

"I asked Tucker, and he asked around and found out about the show. I took a picture of 'Blue Moon Garden' and sent it in. I forged your signature, by the way. Hope you don't mind."

After my first and only art exhibit, which had been a disaster, I'd thrown away most of my work, but Jerry had rescued "Blue Moon Garden." It was hanging in the living room at home. I didn't know what to say.

"Mac?" He sounded worried. "Are you still there? Look, if you don't want to do it, you don't have to. But they accepted you. That oughta count for something."

Actually, it counted for a great deal.

"Don't be angry," he said. "I thought it might give you the push you need."

"I'm not angry." I really wasn't. I should be used to this kind of thing from him by now. "I didn't realize how sneaky you were."

"Oh, I can be much sneakier. So you'll do it?"

"That's three paintings I have to have done by Monday after next."

"Two. You can count 'Blue Moon Garden.'"

That made things a little easier. "Okay, two, but I have a case to consider, as well." I checked my watch. "I've got to meet Shana. We'll have a talk later. A long talk."

AT NOON, I MET Shana at Deely's Burger World, our local burger place. Shana Amry is better known as Shana Fairbourne, author of several steamy historical romance novels where words like "passion" and "desire" figure prominently. A tall graceful woman with red-gold hair and tiger-like yellow eyes, she could easily be the heroine of her novels.

I sat down at Shana's table. She introduced me to the woman sitting beside her. "Madeline, this is Rachel Sigmon. She teaches art at Celosia Elementary. Rachel, Madeline Maclin Fairweather. Madeline's our resident Sherlock Holmes."

Rachel Sigmon was a small, slim woman with shoulder-length black hair and wide brown eyes. Her daisy earrings matched her sundress, and she was wearing an extra little cuff high on the edge of her right ear. This piece also had a daisy dangling from a tiny chain. "Hello, Madeline, nice to meet you."

"Nice to meet you, too," I said. "I like your ear jewelry. Did you make it?"

She touched the cuff. "You mean this? Yes, I did. I have this odd little notch in my ear, and this covers it nicely. I made the earrings, too."

"I've often told her she should start her own line," Shana said.

"Oh, but I'm not here to talk earrings," Rachel Sigmon said. "Madeline, I saw the portrait you did for the theater lobby. Would you be willing to come show my classes some portrait techniques?"

I turned to glare at Shana. She was pretending to examine her perfect fingernails. "I'm not a teacher."

"Oh, I'm not asking for a complete lesson plan. The kids would enjoy seeing a real artist at work."

I'm not a real artist, I started to say, and since Jerry wasn't there to kick me under the table, I gave myself a mental kick. Yes, you are! You've got to start believing that. You're going to be in a show!

"You know," Rachel said, "I've seen art change children's lives. Sometimes art is the only thing in which some of them can excel. Maybe they can't do math, or have poor reading skills, but they can draw. You'd be amazed how it builds their confidence."

And isn't that what you need? I asked myself. A big shot of confidence?

"Okay," I said.

"Great! How about tomorrow?"

"Tomorrow?"

"Unless you're busy with your cases?"

Well, I certainly wasn't busy with cases. I had one lone riddle to solve. Might as well jump right in. "Sure. Tomorrow's fine."

"Great! Come around one o'clock. I'll have all the materials for you. Just show the kids how you start with a sketch and then go from there."

"I think I can do that."

Rachel spent the rest of the lunch talking about her daughters, Bronwen and Magwen. Shana avoided making eye contact with me. I could tell she was having difficulty keeping her laughter inside. She knows I have a thing about little girls' names. With so many lovely names to choose from, I am often astounded by the choices people make. Exhibit A: Darlan Kyle, who may or may not be female. Shana also knows how I feel about children. I'm pretty sure her young husband,

Hayden, fulfills her need to have a child. And, as I've indicated, Jerry has more than his share of childlike tendencies.

"So Bron has three dances in the recital, and Mag has two. They wanted to go to cheerleading camp, but I told them they had to choose. They couldn't do cheerleading and dance. They're both Girl Scouts, so we don't have time for another activity. I was so pleased when they decided to continue their dance lessons. Of course, whatever Bron does, Mag wants to do, too."

Bron and Mag. Good grief.

"Did I show you their latest pictures, Shana?"

"Yes," she said with a smile of pure innocence, "but I don't believe Madeline has seen them."

I'll get you for this, Shana Amry. I put on my most interested expression and made all the right comments about Rachel's little girls, who sadly had not inherited their mother's looks. In every photo, they looked round and glum, squinting in the sunlight, their expressions annoyed, as if they resented having their pictures taken.

"What do you think about putting them in a Little Miss Pageant, Madeline? They've asked me about it. I think Bron would do well. She's more outgoing. But Mag's the better actress."

"I wouldn't advise it," I said.

Rachel looked surprised. "Really? I thought you won several Little Miss titles."

"All my mother's idea."

"Oh, you were pushed into it? See, I'm not like that, at all. The girls want to do it."

I'd heard that excuse a thousand times. "Wait until

they're teenagers. Then they'll know what they're getting into."

"What do you think, Shana?"

"You might want to wait until the girls are older," Shana said.

Rachel Sigmon was one of those people who ask for your opinion but never really want it. "Oh, I think it'll be fun. They love to dress up."

She chatted on about her daughters until she had to go pick Bronwen up at her dance lesson. As soon as she was gone, I leveled my darkest look at Shana. "You'll pay for that."

She laughed. "Which part? Having to look at her pictures, listen to her gush, or talk to her class?"

"All three, but the last one in particular. I thought she might have a case for me."

"You're not hoping for another murder, are you?"

"Of course not. I'm very good at finding lost umbrellas, too."

Shana laughed again. A lost umbrella had made an effective weapon when a murderous woman had attacked me in the library. "I'm sorry. I'll try to find something more lurid next time."

"How's Hayden's work coming along?"

"He's doing very well. He actually finished a poem yesterday, one very nice elegant, incomprehensible poem."

"And your latest?"

"I'm up to page four hundred and thirty-four. And how's Jerry? He looks like he's having a good time at the store."

"Oh, he's having a good time, all right. He's entered me in an art show in Parkland."

"Really? Are you going to do it?"

"I've got to find time to finish two paintings."

She smiled. "Are you a little annoyed with him?"

"Just a little. Now that I'm over the shock, I have to agree I never would have entered on my own."

"So aside from Jerry's schemes, how's married life?"

I had to admit it was great fun.

"And the wedding? I hear you ran away to the beach."

"The Fairweather family has a beach house in Bermuda."

"How convenient."

"I enjoyed it much more this time. The last time I was there, I was recovering from my one and only art show."

"Oh, yes, the disaster." She gave me a long considering look. "Then it's time for another one, isn't it? Another show, I mean, not another disaster. This show will be perfect. Any idea what's holding you back?"

"Well, I'd like to say I'm swamped with cases, but I just have one."

"Maybe Celosia is too small."

"I really don't want to move back to Parkland. It's too big."

"You might want to consider Rossboro, then."

Rossboro was home to Elijah's lawyer, Misty May. I started to ask Shana about the town when Annie, one of the waitresses, stopped by to refill our tea glasses. "Anything else for you ladies?"

"No, thanks," we said.

"I'm halfway through *Total Surrender,* Shana," she said. "It's wonderful. I love the scene where Vixen tells

Slate he's not the only man for her. She's just saying that, isn't she? She doesn't really mean it. He really is the only man for her."

"She's going through a rough time," Shana said. "You know how it is when you have to make a tough decision."

"I'll say! We're wanting to add another flavor of milkshake to the menu, and trying to figure out what kind is driving us all crazy. What do you think? Banana or blueberry?"

"Oh, I vote for banana."

"Me, too," I said.

"That's what I want. Nobody really likes blue drinks, you know." She tore our bill off her pad and put it on the table. "Thanks, girls."

"Decisions, decisions," I said. "Banana or blueberry? Slate or—who is it? Dirk?"

"Yes. Dirk Steel."

"Dirk Steel." I snickered, and Shana pretended to be offended.

"It's a difficult choice."

"Now what's this about Rossboro? I just called a lawyer's office there."

"It's larger than Celosia, but not as large as Parkland. I'm not trying to get rid of you, you understand, but there might be more work for you. It's only about forty minutes from here. We could take a little road trip."

"That sounds like fun."

Shana set her elbows on the table, laced her fingers, and propped her chin on her hands. "So. What's really holding you back from showing your work?"

I sighed. "Fear, of course. Fear of failure. Fear of ridicule. The usual."

"But you faced Chance Baseford, the man who critiqued your first show. You said you felt good after that encounter."

"Oh, I did. But he's not my worst critic. I am."

"Well, you'll never know if you don't give it another try."

"That's true." I was surprised by my growing feelings of excitement. The gallery had liked "Blue Moon Garden." Why wouldn't they like my other paintings? Paintings, however, I hadn't done. Suppose they liked those, too? Suppose they said, let's have an exhibit of your work. And those pieces sold, and I had more commissioned, and more shows, and I tuned back in time to hear Shana say, "So tell me more about the wedding. What did you wear? Did you get married on the beach?"

"Yes. I had a very nice flowing flowery dress, and Jerry wore a white shirt and pants and, in honor of the solemn occasion, a white tie with golden flying fish on it. We left our shoes on the porch."

"Any guests?"

"Jerry's brothers, Des and Tucker, and Tucker's new wife, Selene. My mother wasn't very happy."

"She didn't really expect to be invited, did she?"

"Oh, I invited her, but she decided not to come. She was upset to learn that Jerry still doesn't want any of the Fairweather money."

"Does Jerry need something more to do? Maybe working in the bookstore's not enough of a challenge."

"He still holds séances."

"You're kidding."

"Flossie Mae Snyder and Sylvie come faithfully every week to talk to their dead aunts."

"Well, if they're silly enough to believe him."

"I thought once I solved the mystery of his parents' deaths he'd stop the paranormal stuff." For years Jerry felt responsible for the fire that killed his parents, but I'd pieced together the real story. "He and his older sister Harriet are on good terms now, and he's even visited Tucker at the family home."

"He may need a little more time to adjust, that's all. Which opera is he listening to these days?"

Jerry liked opera, and his choice usually mirrored his mood. *"The Tales of Hoffmann."*

"I don't know that one."

"Oh, he's dragged me to it many times. The opera's an odd mix of three fantasy stories. One story's about a mechanical doll, one's about a woman who sings herself to death, and one story takes place in Venice, where Hoffmann's soul is stolen by a beautiful courtesan. The character of Hoffmann was a restless man searching for the ideal woman, embodied by those three very different characters. He ends up drunk and alone."

Shana shook her head. "Okay, I have no idea what that could mean."

"Me, either," I said.

I COULDN'T WAIT to have that long talk with my husband, so after leaving Shana, I stopped by Georgia's Books. Jerry was helping Austin and Denisha sort through packs of Bufo cards. As usual, the kids were arguing about proper procedure.

"You need to pick a pack from the bottom, Denisha. That's where all the best cards come from."

"Austin Terrell, don't you think I know that? Besides, if other kids have already been through the packs, the ones that used to be on the bottom are now on the top."

"How are we ever going to complete our set if you don't hurry up?"

They finally reached a settlement and dumped their change on the counter.

"Do you have enough?" I asked.

"Yes, thanks," Austin answered.

Denisha dug in the pocket of her shorts for another quarter. "I have more money right here. Go ahead, Austin."

Jerry handed him the cards. I don't know who was more excited, the kids or Jerry as Austin tore off the green foil and quickly flipped through the cards. He held one up in triumph. "The Lily Pad!"

Denisha grabbed his hand. "Let me see! It's the white one! Now we've got all three."

I looked to Jerry for enlightenment. "The Lily Pads come in white, yellow, and pink," he said. "Open another pack, Austin."

The other packs yielded the Horned Toad of Death, the Evil Frog Prince, and a pile of other lesser cards.

"I'm getting a new shipment soon," Jerry said. "We'll try again."

After Austin and Denisha left, I gave Jerry a look.

"That's very good," he said. "I see you've perfected the Long Stare."

"You're lucky I've had time to think about this."

"Then you know it's a great idea." Before I could

answer, he said, "I know, I know, my methods were less than legal, but there was a deadline for the application, and I didn't think I could talk you into it before that time was up. Now you can decide if you want to go through with it."

"If I can get two more paintings done by Monday."

"Of course you can. I've had a peek in your studio. There's a picture of the house and one of the kids and even one of me that's already a masterpiece."

I laughed and gave him a kiss. "I'll give it a shot."

"Great! I knew you would. Did Shana have a case for you?"

"She wanted me to meet her friend, Rachel Sigmon. Get this: her daughters are named Bronwen and Magwen."

He made a face. "That's attractive. Our daughter will be named something much more pleasant, like Hortensia."

"Exactly."

"So her friends can call her Horry."

"A cute nickname is always a plus."

"Did Rachel want you to find something for her, aside from a new baby name book?"

"She wants me to talk to her classes about art."

Jerry brightened. "That's encouraging."

"What?"

"That you now have a reputation as an artist as well as an ace detective."

"I suppose," I said. "I'm a little nervous about talking to a group of fourth graders."

"They'll love you. All the little girls will want to look like you, and all the little boys will be dazzled."

"You are the only boy I like to dazzle. When we get home tonight, there's a riddle you can help me solve."

"Okay," he said, "but I have a séance at nine."

The gleam in his eye made my heart sink. "Are you still leading Flossie Mae and her niece on about that watch?"

He tried to look offended. "We're very close to finding it."

"You are not. You're making things up as you go along and you know it."

"But Flossie Mae and Sylvie are having such a good time."

Flossie Mae Snyder and her niece Sylvie had been coming to the house for weeks so Jerry could get in touch with Aunt Marge and Aunt Marie. In life, the two aunts had fought bitterly over a gold watch engraved with an "S." In death, according to Jerry, Marge and Marie had reconciled and any day now would reveal the whereabouts of the watch. I had to admit that Flossie Mae and Sylvie thoroughly enjoy their trips to the Other World, but Jerry's act was getting on my nerves.

"How long are you going to keep this up?" Why did I ask this question? As long as Flossie Mae pays him, he'll keep pretending to talk to Marge and Marie. "You're going to have to disappoint them."

"Or Marge and Marie could come through with the watch."

He can say things like this with a totally straight face. I started to say things he didn't want to hear when Fiona Kittering came into the store. Fiona's a small dark-haired woman who works at Holiday Travel across the street from the bookstore. With her sharp little nose and determined manner, she reminds me of a rat ter-

rier who's out to convince the world she's the biggest
dog in the neighborhood.

"Madeline, did Nathan Fenton come see you this
morning?"

"Yes, he did."

"Good. I told him to."

"Thanks."

"We've been going out for a couple of weeks now,
and he mentioned this inheritance and how he needed
some help with the riddle. I told him you were pretty
good at solving mysteries."

"Thank you," I said.

"Did he mention Chateau Marmot?"

"No."

"I didn't think he would. You need to go to Chateau
Marmot."

"Isn't a marmot something like a groundhog?" Jerry
asked.

I thought I knew all the landmarks around Celosia.
"He mentioned a family home. Where's this chateau?
I've never heard of it."

Fiona pointed out the bookstore window to the left.
"Down that way on Satterfield Drive. It's not far from
here. Nathan's cousin Aaron used to live there, but he
and Victoria are separated. She never speaks to anyone."

"Then what makes you think she'll speak to me?"

"Well, it's a worth a try. You're new in town, so you
don't have any preconceived notions about some of the
older families."

"What can you tell me about the Fenton family?"

She leaned against the counter and folded her arms.
"Well, there were three Fentons. Elijah was the old-

est, then Ellis, and then their sister, Eulalie. Ellis was Nathan's father. Eulalie married Thomas Satterfield. They had a son named Aaron, who married Victoria Dewey—only she was known as Tori then."

"Nathan and Aaron are cousins."

"That's right. I don't know a whole lot about Tori, though. She and Aaron got married and moved into the chateau. He moved out, and I don't think I've seen her since then."

"Nathan hasn't been back to the family home?"

"I honestly don't know all the details. She refuses to talk to him, and she certainly wouldn't talk to me. That's why he hired you."

I wondered why Nathan hadn't told me these important details about his family and the chateau. "Okay, what about the rest of the riddle? What's this about a river and a sparrow?"

"The only river around here is Parson's Creek. As for the sparrow, your guess is as good as mine."

"I understand Uncle Elijah was fond of word games."

"He was an evil old coot. Ask anyone. Nathan says he was always rude to Tori. I guess he didn't like the idea of his nephew Aaron marrying a Dewey. The Deweys weren't on the same social level."

"But he left her the house and some money."

"Because he loved the chateau and knew she would stay there."

"And Aaron's in Parkland."

"Oh, he left Celosia years ago. I don't think he was very kind to Tori. She was probably glad to see him go. Aaron might be able to shed some light on this riddle. Then again, he might not want to help. He and Nathan are quite different." She straightened from the counter and gave her clothes a brief tug to make sure everything was in line. "I tell you, Madeline, Nathan is a fine man. Good manners, educated, and this dream of his to open Camp Lakenwood for underprivileged kids—what a wonderful thing. That's why it's so important we find his fortune."

I noticed she said "we." "Then I hope Mrs. Satterfield will agree to talk to me."

"I think she will. I understand you're an artist, and Tori's somewhat of an artist herself."

Jerry grinned at me. "Notice this is another connection to art."

"The chateau's full of old pictures," Fiona said. "One of them's bound to be the portrait in the riddle."

Nathan hadn't mentioned this, either.

"Is this the riddle you wanted me to see?" Jerry asked.

I took the paper out of my pocket. "There's not a lot to it."

Jerry read the riddle and frowned. "It doesn't make much sense."

"That's why you need to go to the chateau," Fiona said. "I'll bet all the answers are in there."

"How do I get in touch with Mrs. Satterfield? Is Chateau Marmot listed in the phone book?"

"1-800-Rodent," Jerry said.

"I have it with me," Fiona said. She reached in her pocket and handed me a piece of paper. "Here you go."

"Thanks."

"And thank you for helping Nathan. He didn't want to come to you. I think he's embarrassed by the whole thing—oh, not that you're a woman detective. Having

Elijah Fenton for an uncle is embarrassment enough. He must have been a real butthead."

"I'm glad to be on the case," I said. I was glad to be on any case.

Fiona thanked me and left. Jerry took the riddle. "Leave this with me. I'll see what I can figure out."

"I'm going to call Mrs. Satterfield," I said.

I went to the small room at the back of the store the employees used for a break room and took out my cell phone. I was expecting a harsh rebuff, but Victoria Satterfield had a light little feathery voice that trembled with excitement.

"I would very much like to meet you, Ms. Maclin. Could you come tomorrow morning?"

"That would be fine."

"It's the large stone house on Satterfield Drive. Well, actually, it's the only house on Satterfield Drive. Just ring the front doorbell."

"I'll see you then." That was puzzling, I thought. She sounded very pleasant. As I closed my phone, Georgia came in, her arms full of magazines.

"Oh, hello, Madeline." She plopped the magazines on the small table.

"I just stepped back here to make a phone call," I said.

"Anytime, dear." She took off her half glasses and let them dangle on their pearl chain. "Actually, I wanted to talk to you."

Another case? I was pleased and appalled at the same time. When would I find time to paint? "Nothing serious, I hope."

"Well, it depends on how you look at it. Business is a little slow right now, and as much as I love having

Jerry around, there's just not enough for him to do. I'm going to have to cut back on his hours."

Uh-oh. "Business picks up around October, though, doesn't it?"

"Usually. How do you think he'll feel about this?"

I knew exactly how Jerry would feel. Free! Free, at last! "He'll be okay." Oh, my gosh, I'd have to find something for him to do.

"I'm sure I'll have more work for him during the holiday season, but I have to keep my other workers on the payroll. They've been with me for years." She peered at me anxiously. "This isn't going to be a financial burden on you, is it?"

"No, we'll manage," I said. "I have a case right now."

"Good. I was worried. I wanted to sort of find out how things were before I told him."

"He'll be fine, Georgia."

"I think I'll go ahead and let him know today."

My mind whirled with this information as I walked back to the counter. Jerry was laughing and joking with two women who'd been in the community theater's recent production of *The Music Man*.

"Are you going to play for *South Pacific* next summer?" one asked.

"I don't know," he said. "It's hard to plan that far in advance."

"Would you be interested in playing for our Christmas cantata?" the other woman asked. "We're desperate to find somebody. The music isn't hard. I'll bet you could sight-read it."

"I've never played for a church program," he said.

"Oh, it's easy. It's basically lots of Christmas carols

with a few extra tunes thrown in. Why don't I bring a copy by and let you look at it? Then you can decide."

"Okay," he said.

"This might work into a good job for you," she said. "Do you play the organ, too?"

"Never tried that."

"Think about it."

Jerry needed plenty to do, but I knew he didn't want to be tied down every Sunday. He told the women he'd look over the cantata, but he couldn't make any promises. After the women left, there were a few more customers, and then Georgia came up.

"Jerry, dear, I hate to tell you this, but I'm going to have to cut back on your hours. You're a very good worker, but business is slow, and the other employees have been with me for years. I'm just going to need you a few hours every day, if that's all right."

I saw the gleam in Jerry's eyes. "That's fine with me."

"You're sure?"

"Georgia, there are all kinds of things I can do."

She looked relieved. "I'm glad to hear that. I'll have a new schedule for you tomorrow."

"Okay," Jerry said. "See you tomorrow, then. Ready to go, Mac?"

"All set." I kept my smile in place for Georgia's sake, but as we walked down the sidewalk to the car, I said, "I'm a little concerned about this."

"Don't worry. I'll find another job."

"Seriously?"

"You're going to enter the art show, aren't you? We have a deal here."

"Yes, but what sort of job do you have in mind?"

"Oh, something will come up."

"You're not bored here, are you?"

"No, not at all."

"We could always take a trip somewhere, do something a little more exciting."

"Don't worry about me. I can make my own excitement."

"That's what I'm afraid of."

He grinned. "I seem to recall we made a bargain not long ago. I've kept my end of it. I am legally employed. You were supposed to continue your art work, right, Mrs. Fairweather?"

"Yes, and the minute we get home, I'm going to see what can be done." In fact, I'd been anxious to get to my studio. My fingers were practically itching to hold a brush or pencil. "I can't neglect Nathan's case, though."

"It's not a very huge case, is it?"

"Shana suggested I might find more work in another town."

"You want to move?"

"No, just commute. Maybe to Rossboro. Know anything about it?"

"Oh, Jeff and I did Rossboro."

"I'll bet you did."

"The knife trick."

"You weren't throwing knives at each other, were you?"

"No, you set a knife point up and cover it with a paper cup. Then you turn away and have the mark—excuse me, the audience member—put three more paper cups on the table, and you slam your hand down on the ones without the knife. It's very exciting."

"Ow. I'm glad I never saw you do that one."

"It's very easy if you know the secret."

"How long were you in Rossboro before you were chased out?"

"Long enough. It's a nice town. Bigger than Celosia, but most towns are."

"I think I want to have a look."

"Okay."

I felt a little guilty. After all, I'd convinced Jerry to settle down, something I never thought he'd do. He liked the house. I liked the house. If I found work in Rossboro, or anywhere else, a long commute would quickly get old. Well, it was too soon to start worrying about this.

"Do you remember if there were any museums or art galleries?"

"A forger I knew worked in the museum."

I wasn't going to ask.

"When do you want to go scope it out?" Jerry asked.

"Some time soon. Shana's already suggested a road trip, but you can come, too."

"Ride with the most beautiful woman in town?" He paused just long enough. "And Shana? Great! I'm there."

"We might leave you home."

On the drive home, Jerry put in a CD. I recognized the "Barcarole" from *The Tales of Hoffmann*. It's a slow, sensual duet that flows along like the gentle rocking of a gondola. I heard this tune a lot in college. Jerry liked to listen to it just before an important exam.

He took the piece of paper out of his pocket. "I need inspiration for this riddle you gave me."

"Got it solved yet?"

"I wonder what it means by a sparrow from ancient times."

"A really old bird?"

"I looked up 'sparrow,' in the store, thinking it might have another meaning. Here's what Mister Webster says, 'Any of several small dull singing birds.'"

"That's harsh. Not only are they small, but they're dull." He turned the music down a little. "When are you going to Chateau Groundhog?"

"I called and set up an appointment for tomorrow morning."

"So she's really going to see you?"

"I guess being an artist has its uses."

"You're using the power, the power isn't using you."

I leaned over and gave him a kiss. "Thank you."

He looked at the riddle again. "How much money will Fenton get if he solves this riddle?"

"He didn't say. But if he doesn't solve the riddle, all the money goes to—and you're going to love this—building bat houses."

He laughed. "You're kidding."

"Elijah and Val must have been pals."

"Sounds like they were drinking buddies." Jerry folded the riddle back into his pocket. "I'm glad to know I'm not the only one with a screwy uncle." He dug into his other pocket. "We got a new shipment of Bufo cards in today. I had to beat the crowds back with a stick. Want a sticker? I thought I'd decorate the kitchen."

"No, thanks. I have enough to do for tonight."

Besides reviewing my own paintings, I needed to work on some sort of presentation for Rachel's class, so when we got home, I said, "I'm going to do some art stuff now, so don't give me any more grief." I was halfway up the stairs when I heard the steady hum of the fan. "Didn't Nell fix the air conditioner?"

"She called and said she needed a part. She'll be by tomorrow."

Nell Brenner's our resident handywoman. She said she'd always wanted to get her hands on the Eberlin house. I think she got more than she bargained for. She certainly has her hands full with all the repairs the old house needs. When Jerry and I first saw the house, Jerry was delighted by its spooky appearance, but I was appalled by its rundown condition. We soon realized most of the scabbiness was on the outside. Jerry's Uncle Val hadn't felt the need to mow or paint, but he lived very simply. We didn't find clutter or piles of clothes and food wrappers. Inside, the rooms had been bare and dusty with Victorian style furniture. Now the hardwood floors were shiny and the high ceilings free of cobwebs. The kitchen needed just a little updating. We kept the sturdy white wood cabinets and wooden table and chairs. Most of the upstairs bedrooms just needed a paint job, and with Jerry's unwanted assistance, Nell transformed the living room into a calm blue room with a white sofa and crystal lamps. Jerry hung the rescued "Blue Moon Garden" over the mantel.

I needed two more pictures to go with "Blue Moon Garden" to the Weyland Gallery. I checked by my parlor studio. Tacked to my easel was Austin's latest offering, a pencil drawing of an impossibly big wheeled car with a forest of huge tailpipes jutting out behind and a grill like a shark's grin. Denisha hadn't shown an interest in art, but Austin had notebooks filled with detailed sketches of fantasy cars, motorcycles, dinosaurs, and spaceships. I decided I wouldn't mind showing kids how to draw. I'd helped Austin with perspective and shading. I could start with some simple shapes and explain the same concepts to Rachel Sigmon's class.

I sat down for a moment in one of Uncle Val's beautiful old Victorian chairs. I had coveted this room from the beginning. The size and shape, the light, everything was perfect for a studio. I had all my art supplies neatly arranged and lately, I'd had plenty of time to paint. Now that I'd confronted the critic who made my first and only exhibit a nightmare, I felt much more confident in my work, but I wasn't sure I was ready for another show. And what could I possibly use for the New Artists Show?

Propped along the walls of the parlor were my ongoing projects: a landscape of the fields and trees in front of the house, some small drawings of wildflowers, a couple of abstracts, Austin and Denisha holding Austin's boxer puppy, and Jerry's portrait, which was only a rough pencil sketch. Still, I'd manage to capture the sparkle in his gray eyes and a hint of his smile. I'd drawn him leaning over the front porch railing, his head turned toward me, his impish expression suggesting I'd just caught him planning some grand scheme. Okay, so it wouldn't take a lot of work to finish that, and maybe I could use the landscape, if I added more light and color. Of course, there was another painting I'd started of the fields in front of the house that would be a perfect complement to "Blue Moon Garden" if I could get it ready in time.

I looked around the parlor, imaging all the paintings framed and hanging on the walls of an art gallery or museum. I needed to prove to myself that I was a legitimate artist. But the cost of framing, hiring a hall, publicity—I'd have to solve several cases for some very wealthy people before an exhibit was possible, but this Weyland Gallery show was a huge first step toward making this dream a reality.

And you have a case, I told myself. If you help Nathan Fenton get his fortune, who knows? He might be willing to sponsor you. At least he paid his fee. At least you don't have to hold fake séances like your husband. Of course, if I had my way about it, this would be the last fake séance he would hold.

By the time Flossie Mae Snyder and her niece, Sylvie, arrived promptly at nine, I'd made a lot of progress on the fields painting and decided that was enough for tonight. Jerry had a table and chairs arranged in the middle of the parlor and several fat candles glowing. Flossie Mae does not look like the kind of woman who'd believe in talking to the dead or anything paranormal. She's a tall, thin woman with a stern demeanor. Sylvie, who is plump and excitable, looks exactly like the kind of woman who'd believe in ghosts. There must be something in Jerry's performances that enthralls them, because they keep coming back for more.

"Let's see what Aunt Marie and Aunt Marge have to say tonight," he said as they took their places around the table. "Mac, would you mind getting the lights, please?"

I sighed and turned off the parlor lights. Jerry, Flossie Mae, and Sylvie held hands. Jerry closed his eyes and took some long deep breaths. "I call to the spirit world. I request your guidance. Come to me. Show me the way." After a while, he spoke in a distant voice. "I am here."

Sylvie was almost bouncing in her chair. "It's us, Aunt Marie!"

"This is your Aunt Marge, my child."

"Sorry, Aunt Marge. We wanted to know about the watch."

"The watch. Yes, my child. Soon we will reveal the door."

"Door?" Flossie Mae said. "What do you mean?"

Yes, Jerry. Where are you going with this?

"The door that leads to understanding," he said.

"Understanding what?"

"To find what you seek."

"There's a door somewhere?"

Jerry made a funny gargling noise that made Flossie Mae gasp. "The spirits are restless," he said in his faraway voice. "Let me try again."

Flossie Mae and Sylvie sat absolutely still. When Jerry opened his eyes, the women jumped.

"I'm sorry," he said. "There's a lot of confusion in the spirit world tonight. Did Marge or Marie come through?"

"Marge did," Flossie Mae said. "She mentioned something about a door to understanding."

He nodded. "Sometimes the spirits speak in their own language, and we have to figure out what they mean. Is there a door in your house or in one of their houses you haven't tried?"

"Oh!" Sylvie said. "Flossie Mae, that little door that goes out to the porch Uncle Ray boarded up. Have we been out there?"

"There's nothing out there but trash and spiders."

"Maybe we ought to look."

"Well, all right. It's worth a try, I suppose."

Jerry saw them to the door. Sylvie chatted on about how it was always such a thrill to talk to her aunts. Flossie Mae tried to hand him some money, but he folded the bills back into her hand.

"This one's on the house, Mrs. Snyder."

"Thank you, but we really should pay you for your services."

"How 'bout you pay me when we find the watch? It won't be long now."

"Very well. But I'll insist you take half of whatever the watch is worth."

"Well, that was nice," I said, after Flossie Mae and Sylvie had gone. "But they're never going to find a watch that doesn't exist."

"Have a little faith. All I have to do is go into Parkland and find a big gold watch with an 'S' on it and make it magically appear during a séance."

"And how are you going to pay for this big gold watch? Aren't they expecting it to be worth a lot of money?"

"I'm working on that." He blew out the candles and moved the table and chairs back to one side of the parlor. Then he said, "Were you serious about little Horry?"

His question took me by surprise. "What?"

"Earlier today, when we were talking about girls' names. You want to have a Hortensia?"

Where was all this coming from? "Sure, and a Dorcas and an Ermintrude and a Trumilla."

"Seriously."

Seriously? Jerry was rarely serious about anything. I tried to keep things light. "But we already have two children, one of each."

"Those are on loan. Do you want kids?"

"We've had this talk."

"Yeah, but we're married now. That might make a difference."

"Not to me," I said.

"Okay."

I could tell he wanted to say something else. "How important is it to you?"

"It's not," he said. "I just thought you might have changed your mind."

"No, I haven't."

But later that night, as I lay curled up next to Jerry in bed, my head on his shoulder and my hand on his chest, listening to him sleep, I wondered, as I had many times before, what our children would be like. I had finally married my best friend, and our relationship was stronger than ever. I'd always said I didn't want children, but now that I had someone who would be a wonderful father, maybe I should reconsider.

No, I thought as I snuggled in closer. I had all I wanted right here.

TWO

THE NEXT MORNING, I got up early and worked on the sketch of Jerry. I didn't want to add too much, so I spent a lot of time looking at the drawing from all angles, pondering what to do. Finally I decided not to do any more. Maybe the painting of the kids and the dog would be a better choice. Or maybe it would be too commercial. I went round and round arguing with myself until it was time to go to Chateau Marmot.

Satterfield Drive was a long driveway that wound through pine trees and bushes in need of a good trim. Then the road circled a dry stone fountain and stopped in front of a tremendous house. The chateau was made of plain gray ivy-covered stone with a tower on each side. The windows were dark, and for a moment, I thought no one was home. I didn't see any other cars, so I parked the Mazda beside a sad-looking stone planter filled with weeds. I rang the doorbell beside the huge wooden door and heard chimes echo in the distance. In a few minutes, the door opened.

"Victoria Satterfield" was a name that conjured up images of a haughty patrician dowager. The woman who greeted me was small and frail with huge dark eyes.

"Ms. Maclin? Come in, come in."

I shook her cold little hand, feeling tiny bird-like bones. "It's nice to meet you, Mrs. Satterfield."

"Please call me Tori. Come into my study and have a seat."

For my visit, I had put on my best blue slacks and a white eyelet blouse over a white lace camisole. Tori appeared to be wearing a dress made of brown leaves. She led me down a cold stony hallway to her study. The study was as dark as a cave. Fiona Kittering had said Tori Satterfield was an artist, but I saw no evidence of this. Small flower-shaped lamps burned in the corners and on the little round table. I was almost afraid to sit in the delicate chair, but it held me. Tori perched on the edge of her chair. Her wispy hair strayed from its untidy bun. I could see now that the brown dress was tattered and seemed to camouflage her. She indicated the large pile of newspaper clippings on the table.

"I was just working on my scrapbook."

The table was covered with newspapers, scissors, glue, and scraps of colored foil. Now that my eyes had adjusted to the gloom, I saw the entire room was filled with stacks of newspapers and magazines. Stacked on the bookcases were dozens of scrapbooks crammed full, papers hanging out in all directions.

"You've done a lot of work, Tori."

"Oh, I just love it. My scrapbooks are my passion."

All I could think of was, one spark from a match, and the whole house goes up like a bonfire.

"Are your scrapbooks all about your life?"

Tori hugged her little stick arms. "Oh, my, no. I can't think of anything more boring. They're about ballet. I love the ballet."

"You're a dancer?"

"Well, for a brief time I was." She dragged one of the scrapbooks off the shelf and heaved it onto the table. Bits of dust and yellowed paper billowed up as she turned the pages. "Here I am."

The photograph showed a younger beaming Tori dressed in a white tutu and carrying a bouquet of roses as big as she was. Also on the page was a program trimmed with pink candy and silver stars.

"Very nice," I said.

"When I was sixteen, I was Clara in *The Nutcracker* for the Parkland Ballet. The happiest day of my life."

As she looked at the picture, her expression was anything but happy. It was the most melancholy expression I'd ever seen. If my whole happiness was tied to that one moment, I'd be melancholy, too, I thought, wondering what had happened to change that radiant girl in the picture into this fragile little woman hiding among stacks of old newspapers. According to the date on the program, Tori had been sixteen twenty years ago, which made her a surprisingly young thirty-six, about Nathan's age. I'd first thought she was older.

"Tori, may I ask you about your husband?"

She sighed. "He decided he didn't want to live here any more."

"I'm very sorry."

"Oh, in a way, I guess it's better. The Fentons never accepted me, and that made him mad, but he took his anger out on me. I never understood that. I don't know what I could've done to make things better."

"Your husband's cousin, Nathan, asked me to help solve a riddle Elijah Fenton left as a clue to Nathan's inheritance. Do you know anything about that?"

"No." Tori closed the scrapbook. Her little hand lingered on the cover. "I gave up my dance career when I married Aaron. I don't think he ever understood why

I liked it so much. He never wanted to go to the ballet with me. After a while, he never wanted to go anywhere with me."

"I'm sorry. Do you go to Parkland to see the ballet?"

"No. That's where Aaron is, and I don't want to see him." She sighed. "They did a wonderful Copelia last season, though. I read all about it. I have all the reviews in one of my scrapbooks. Let's see." She pulled another scrapbook from the stacks and looked through the wide pages. "Here. I did this whole section in green and yellow to match their costumes."

Perhaps this was what Fiona meant by art. Tori had used pinking shears to create a rick rack border around the newspaper articles and lined the border with shiny green and yellow paper.

"This season they're doing *Sleeping Beauty*. I know it's going to be amazing. I'm thinking of using that silver foil, the kind you see on Christmas wrapping with little rainbow highlights. I don't know what it's called."

"Hologram?"

"Yes, with all the colors. And I've got all different kinds of lace for borders. You're an artist, too, I understand. What kind of art do you create?"

"Paintings mostly, some pen and ink and pencil drawings, abstracts, landscapes."

"I have a clipping from the *Celosia News* about the picture you did for the theater." Again she dug into the stacks and found the book she wanted. She searched its pages and pointed proudly at the clipping. "I thought this was such a wonderful picture."

The theater had asked me to paint a group of children in costumes. Their faces beamed up from the article. Tori had decorated this page with little balloons. "Thank you."

"Well, I could talk about my scrapbooks all day, but that's not why you've really come, is it?"

She didn't sound angry, just disappointed. "Maybe you could help me solve this riddle," I said. "Are there any portraits in your house?"

"Quite a few."

"Would you mind if I looked behind them?"

"I don't have any hidden safes behind pictures."

"I don't think the answer is in a safe."

"You're certainly welcome to look." She brightened. "This could be like a treasure hunt."

"Yes, that's exactly what it is."

"I've always wanted to go on a treasure hunt. So there might be something valuable behind one of the portraits?" she asked as she led me to the main hallway.

"It's possible. The riddle says, 'And listen where the portrait lies.'"

When I saw the long hall, I stopped. The walls on both sides were covered with pictures in huge ornate frames. Tori gave me an apologetic look. "The Satterfields and the Fentons were rather proud of themselves."

I was going to need some help, and little Tori was much too frail to lift even the smallest pictures. "Do you mind if I come back and bring my husband to help me?"

"Not at all."

I checked my watch. "Maybe tomorrow about this time?"

"Any time you like." At the front door, she put her little hand on my arm.

"Madeline, I've really enjoyed our visit. It's so nice to talk to a fellow artist."

"I like ballet, too," I said. "Maybe we could go together to see *Sleeping Beauty*."

"Oh, I won't be able to do that."

I thought perhaps her health prevented her from traveling. "I'll be glad to take you."

Her large eyes filled with tears. "That's so kind, but really, it's impossible."

"I realize you don't want to run into Aaron, but it's unlikely he'd be at the ballet, right?"

"I can't go."

I was curious, but I didn't want to pry any further. "All right, but if you change your mind, let me know."

As I drove away, I looked back at the chateau, hoping to see her at the door, but she'd already closed herself in.

I DROVE TO MY OFFICE, and as I was getting out of my car, my cell phone rang. It was Aaron Satterfield.

"Good morning, Ms. Maclin. I understand you wanted to speak to me. How can I help you?"

"I'm a private investigator, Mr. Satterfield, and your cousin, Nathan Fenton, has hired me to help him solve a riddle from your uncle Elijah."

Aaron Satterfield gave a snort of laughter. "Oh, yes. The riddle. I received a copy of it, too, but I've no interest in playing my uncle's little game. He jerked me around enough when I was younger. I'm certainly not going to drop everything and hunt all over the countryside on the off chance I might find some money."

"Even if it's a lot of money?"

Another snort. "My business is doing well enough,

Ms. Maclin. Believe me, I've been the butt of too many of Elijah's jokes to try another. Nathan can tramp through Celosia. I've had enough of that town."

"How long have you been in Parkland?"

"Five years. If you live in Celosia, you probably know the whole story, although I doubt you've met my wife, Tori."

"Actually, I have. I'm sorry about your present situation."

"Yes, well, it didn't work out. We'll probably get divorced. I haven't even seen her since I left. I didn't bother coming back for Elijah's funeral. If he hadn't been such a jerk, Nathan would have some money by now, without having to hire outside help. I think he wants to buy a camp or something?"

"Yes, Camp Lakenwood."

"But the old bastard didn't like anyone having an independent thought, so he decided to play games. He didn't like me marrying Miss Dewey, so he cut me off. Too bad he didn't live to see how well I'm doing without his help or his money. Now he expects me to jump through hoops for a little cash? Good luck to Nathan, I say. If I could help him out, I would."

"Do you have any idea what the riddle means?"

"Sparrows, I don't know. Portraits—there should be some in the chateau. And as for the animals that live in packs, there used to be a pack of wolves that lived in the forest behind the chateau, but that was years ago. I'm sure they're all gone, and what that would mean, I have no idea. I hope you can help him figure it out. Nathan deserves the money. He'll do a lot of good with it, and I can say, 'That fine man there is my cousin.' But I don't think he'll be able to find it."

"Do you know of anyone else who might have received a copy of the riddle?"

"My wife, perhaps. Maybe some of the women Elijah dated. He was a womanizer, even when my aunt was alive. People in Celosia will know, trust me."

I thanked him and closed my phone. Aaron Satterfield seemed genuinely concerned about Nathan's difficulty and unconcerned about the riddle. Then again, he could be planning to join the treasure hunt and didn't want anyone to know.

I went into my office. I had just sat down at my desk when my phone rang again. This time it was Elijah's lawyer, Misty May. She sounded much tougher than her name suggested. I explained that Nathan Fenton had hired me to help solve Elijah's riddle.

"This is what I can tell you, Ms. Maclin," she said. "Elijah Fenton left a legal will, leaving Chateau Marmot to Victoria Satterfield, as well as enough money for the upkeep of the house. The rest of his money he cashed and put in a trust fund. I'm the trustee. Whoever solves the riddle will find a key. If that person brings the key to me, then I give them the money. If no one solves the riddle by Monday, September 23, then I'm to see that his money is used to build bat houses in Celosia. It's a bit nutty, but I've seen worse."

"Do you know how many people have a copy of the riddle?"

"I mailed three letters, but Elijah could've sent more. He never told me exactly how many people he wanted in on his game."

"Does the riddle have to be solved by a particular time on Monday?"

"By midnight, just like all the fairy tales."

I hoped I could make this fairy tale have a happy ending for Nathan Fenton.

AT ONE THAT AFTERNOON, I went to Celosia Elementary and was directed to the art room. Two classes of fourth graders stared up at me as if I were a particularly interesting alien. I'd never seen so many intense expressions. I'd hoped that Austin or Denisha might be in one of these classes, but they weren't.

Rachel introduced me. "Students, this is Mrs. Madeline Maclin Fairweather. She's an artist. You may have seen the picture of the children in costumes she painted for the theater lobby. She's here to show you how to draw faces, and I'm sure she'll answer any questions you may have."

Up went twenty hands.

Rachel called on one large boy in the back. "Ronald?"

"Are you the same lady who whacked Mrs. King on the head with an umbrella?"

Another boy called out, "And aren't you the one who found the Mantis Man and pulled his arm off?"

"Yeah, and squirted old Mrs. Williams with some hairspray right in the face 'cause she was shooting at you?"

Rachel tried to establish order. "Boys and girls, Mrs. Fairweather is here to answer art questions."

I could see "to hell with that" written on their little faces. Ronald waved his arm. "And didn't you find a million dollars in a box?"

"And wasn't there a movie at your house about this guy dying?"

"Isn't Mister Fairweather a warlock? That's what my mom says."

"Boys and girls, only questions about art, please."

Ronald frowned and gave it a try. "Have you ever painted any pictures of dead people?"

Rachel shook her head. "I think that's enough. Why don't we get started on our pictures?"

As she passed out sheets of drawing paper, I drew several faces on the chalkboard and told the students to guess who they were. They laughed as they recognized some of their classmates.

"You see how just a few lines can change the shape of someone's eye, or nose, or ear, or even their chin? This boy's eyebrows go up, but this boy's eyebrows are straight across. See if you can draw my face. I'll try to sit still."

Another girl knocked at the classroom door. "Mrs. Sigmon? You said you wanted to see me at one thirty."

Rachel glanced at the clock. "Oh, yes, thank you. Mrs. Fairweather, please excuse me for a moment. I forgot I told Jennifer to come pick up some pictures for the newspaper contest." She gathered a stack of drawings. The one on top was a brightly colored jungle scene. "Boys and girls, I'll be right back. Please be on your best behavior."

The students were so deeply involved in their sketches, the only sounds I heard were the scratchings of pencils. Then a thin nervous-looking woman came to the door. Light glinted off her glasses as she trembled. "Is Mrs. Sigmon here?"

"She went to the office," I said. "She should be back in a few minutes."

The woman blinked rapidly, as if trying not to cry. "If I could speak to you for a moment out in the hall, then."

We stepped out into the hallway. "Are you a visitor?" the woman asked.

"Yes, I'm Madeline Fairweather. Rachel invited me to speak to the students."

"Well, I'm so sorry to interrupt, but this is an emergency. I'm Mrs. Dorman, Mrs. Lever's assistant. There's been some sort of accident. I think Mrs. Lever's dead. I need to take her class back to their room. I can take Mrs. Petry's class, too."

"Where did this happen?"

"They think she had a heart attack out on the loading deck. That's where our teachers who smoke go for a cigarette."

"Which way to the loading dock?"

She pointed to the right. "Past the cafeteria. The principal just found out and called me. He's gone to find out what happened."

I wanted to know what happened, too.

Mrs. Dorman stepped into the art room. "Boys and girls, we need to go. Mrs. Petry's class, please line up behind Mrs. Lever's class. Mrs. Fairweather will come back another day."

The children groaned but made orderly lines. As soon as they were all gone, I went down the hall and through the cafeteria. A large woman lay stretched out on the loading deck, face white, mouth open as if surprised death had the nerve to pick on her.

Rachel and two other people were on the deck. A middle-aged man bent over Mrs. Lever as if unsure what sort of first aid to administer. Another woman stood to one side looking terrified. She had on a white uniform and hairnet. I assumed she was a cafeteria worker.

"Madeline, did Mrs. Dorman pick up the children?" Rachel asked.

"Yes, she took both classes. What happened?"

"I needed to check with Jacey about helping with an art project. Amelia came out, gasped, and fell over. I sent Jacey to call Thad. I tried CPR, but—" Her voice quit.

Jacey, the woman in the white uniform, was shaking. "I was out here, having a smoke, as usual. Mrs. Lever always comes out and has one about this time, but she acted like she couldn't catch her breath. When she fell over, Mrs. Sigmon said go call the principal, she'd start CPR. I ran and called Mister Murphy, but it was too late."

The man straightened. "I'm Thad Murphy, principal. Are you a doctor?"

"No, I'm Madeline Fairweather. I was visiting Mrs. Sigmon's class. Has anything been moved or rearranged?"

He shook his head. In the distance, we could hear the faint sound of a siren. "I think she had a heart attack. I don't believe we could've saved her. It's all right, Miss Jacey. You can go back in. I'll let you know if we need to talk to you."

Amelia Lever had been a large unattractive woman with bristly gray hair and a prominent nose. Her dark purple lipstick made a garish contrast to her white face. There was a flesh-colored patch on her upper arm. A nicotine patch? Could you wear those and still smoke?

"Was Mrs. Lever trying to quit smoking?" I asked.

The principal pointed to the pile of cigarette butts sticking in a trashcan filled with sand. "I don't think so. Miss Jacey said she lit up before she was out the door. She smoked for about three minutes and then got kind of glassy-eyed and said her heart was racing."

"That looks like a nicotine patch on her arm."

Rachel said, "Could she have overdosed on nicotine? That's possible, isn't it?"

That was something the emergency team said they would suggest after they'd inspected everything and carried Amelia Lever's body away. Thad Murphy turned to me.

"Aren't you Madeline Maclin? I understand you're an investigator."

"Yes, I might be able to help, if you don't mind me asking around."

"Do you think there's something suspicious about Amelia's death?"

"Unless she was suicidal, why would she be smoking while wearing a nicotine patch?"

"I have no idea." He lowered his voice. "I have no objections to you investigating this, but I answer to the school board. They'd have to give permission, and we'd have to officially hire you. This may take some time."

"I understand," I said. "Unofficially, I may be able to gather some information today."

"I know where you can start," Rachel said. "The teachers' lounge."

I thought the Internet was fast, but the teachers' lounge was already buzzing with the news of Amelia's Last Cigarette. Rachel introduced me to everyone at the table. Josh Kellogg, a tall, untidy fifth grade teacher, had a shirt and tie barely containing his belly.

DeAnne Rivers, a third grade teacher, was a small intense woman with short unnaturally red hair. Brenda Mullins, the school nurse, had fluffy blonde hair and a slightly dull expression. I wondered why she hadn't been called to the loading dock and asked her that very question.

"Oh, I just got here," she said. "I work at the high school, too. I missed all the excitement."

Other teachers and assistants rushed in and out, having just enough time to say hello, grab a drink out of the machine and their lunch out of the fridge.

"So you're the one who caught that librarian who killed the movie director," Josh said. "You think someone killed Amelia?"

"I don't know," I said. "She may have overdosed on nicotine."

"Can you believe it?" Brenda Mullins said. "I can't wait to tell Joey."

DeAnne Rivers unwrapped her sandwich. "You should've seen the Doormat's face. I thought she was going to faint."

"She probably did it," Josh Kellogg said. "You gotta watch the quiet ones."

I turned to Rachel. "Doormat?"

"That's our rather unkind nickname for Mrs. Dorman."

"Because she really is a doormat to Amelia Lever— or at least she was," DeAnne said. "Josh, you're just lucky you weren't at the scene of the crime."

"DeAnne, just because the old bag's dead doesn't change how I feel about her. She was one of the meanest bitches I've ever had the misfortune to work with."

She took a bite of sandwich. "It does get you back on the planning committee."

"Hey, I'd forgotten about that. Now that Lever's dead, I move up."

"Uh-oh, I smell a motive. Are you taking notes, Ms. Maclin?"

Josh reached for one of the packs of sugar on the table, opened it, and shook the contents into his coffee. "She only took the committee position because she knew I wanted it."

"And where were you when she keeled over?" DeAnne asked.

"Taking my class to P.E. Where were you?"

"Getting stickers and gum off the computer keyboard." She turned to Rachel. "Who was at the scene of the crime, Rachel?"

"Who's calling it a crime? She never should have been smoking. I went out to speak to Jacey, so it was the two of us."

Josh slurped the last of his coffee. "Rachel could've iced her, couldn't you, Rachel? Amelia's the main reason the arts program didn't get that grant."

"That's not something I'd kill for, Josh."

"I would. The old bat purposely voted against using PTA money for new P.E. equipment, too. She was an equal opportunity miser."

DeAnne had finished her sandwich. She crumpled the wrapping and tossed it in the trashcan. "Let's face it, people. Everyone in this school hated her and isn't sorry she's dead. You've got plenty of suspects, Ms. Maclin. Besides, who says it's murder? She had a heart attack. Maybe we just wish it had been murder."

Josh shrugged. "Who cares? I'm sure the Doormat's

going to be broken up about it. Probably danced all the way down the hall."

"I doubt that," Brenda said. "She's too old."

Kellogg and Rivers exchanged a glance that spoke volumes about their opinion of Brenda Mullins.

"I mean she's glad Lever's dead, Brenda," Josh said.

Brenda still didn't get it. "But Mrs. Dorman wouldn't be dancing, even if she could. The students might see her."

"The students would join right in. 'Ding, dong, the witch is dead.'"

"That's from 'Wizard of Oz.'"

"Correct, Mullins. Ten points to you."

"That's Joey's favorite movie."

I leaned over to Rachel. "Who's Joey?"

"Her boyfriend. He works at the hospital. She talks about him a lot."

Josh grinned at me. "Have you heard enough of our confessions? Get them all straight now. I hated Amelia because she took a committee position that should have been mine, the P.E. teacher hated Amelia because she voted against new equipment, Rachel hated Amelia because she kept the arts program from getting a grant, DeAnne hated Amelia because—why did you hate Amelia, DeAnne?"

"Just on general principles."

"Brenda, why did you hate Amelia?"

"Oh, she was always so rude. Joey says it's because she's old and worn out."

"She's definitely worn out now."

"I understand the universal hatred," I said, "but did she ever threaten anyone's life, or do anything truly serious?"

"No, she was just a miserable old crank."

Thad Murphy stuck his head in the door. "We'll have a brief memorial for Amelia at PTA tonight. I realize she wasn't the easiest person to get along with, but she was a member of this faculty, and I'd like to see some respect."

"Yes, sir," DeAnne said. "Have you found a replacement for her?"

"Norma Olsen's agreed to come in. And Ms. Maclin, if you'd stop by my office, please."

After Murphy left, Josh said, "Didn't Olsen want Lever's job anyway?"

"I heard Amelia purposely didn't retire this year just to spite Norma."

"Uh-oh, another motive."

"Maybe Amelia slept with Hanover."

I didn't get the reference, but everyone laughed except Rachel, who blushed and whispered, "Alan Hanover is our superintendent."

The teachers gathered up their things and left, still laughing.

"Your lunch bunch is a little on the cruel side," I said.

"I suppose they are. You can talk to everyone tonight at PTA," Rachel said. "And I'm sorry if I don't seem very upset, Madeline, but you've just heard what she was like. She never contributed to our Sunshine Fund. She never came to any faculty parties. You had to be careful when you talked to her because she got offended so easily. She was extremely difficult and hard to know. She probably should've retired years ago."

Well, she was retired now.

THAD MURPHY invited me into his office and shut the door. The windows were decorated with children's drawings and cards. The drawings Rachel had given to Jennifer were stacked on his desk. I recognized the bright jungle scene on top.

"I just spoke with the hospital, the superintendent, and two school board members. The doctors have some questions about Mrs. Lever's death. They say it appears she had a heart attack. But I'm concerned about protecting the school and the faculty. I want to make certain Celosia Elementary's reputation is not compromised in any way, and that there was no careless action on anyone's part regarding this incident. I don't want anyone to say we didn't do everything possible to try to save Amelia's life."

"I understand," I said. "It seems to me your first responders did the best they could."

"I want to make sure of that."

"Do you anticipate a problem regarding the fact your school nurse wasn't here?"

"It's common knowledge we share a professional health care provider with the high school. I hope that won't be an issue. That's why ten of our teachers are certified in CPR."

"I have to say the faculty members in the teachers' lounge didn't seem very upset."

He sighed. "Unfortunately, Amelia Lever was not very friendly."

"Isn't that unusual for an elementary school teacher? Didn't parents complain?"

"Yes, we had complaints, and several parents didn't want their children in her class. But that holds true for every single teacher in this school. Many parents liked her more structured ways and didn't have a problem with her abrupt manner."

"What about the students?"

"A few of them were scared of her, but a few are scared of Ms. Mullins, too. Amelia was a good teacher. Her students always scored very high on the end of grade tests."

"How many more years did she have before she retired?"

"She was sixty-nine. She could have retired three years ago."

"Any idea why she kept working?"

"Teachers don't have to retire after thirty years if they don't want to. I assumed she still wanted to teach."

But it sounded to me as if Amelia Lever hated her job. Maybe there were financial concerns. "Was she the sole support of her family?"

"No, her sons work at one of the local clothing mills. Administrative positions, as I understand it. They took over after their father, George Lever, died in a car accident several years ago. I don't think the Levers could be considered poor by any means."

"What about health issues?"

"Aside from smoking, she seemed very healthy. She rarely took a sick day."

"Your teachers have a lot of little grievances against her. Did she have any serious confrontations with other faculty members that might have aggravated a heart condition?"

"Amelia was extremely opinionated. I was often called in to mediate. Believe me, there can be enough stress in the school day to cause more than one heart attack." He glanced at his wrist watch. "I need to talk with her class and make sure everyone's okay. Just stop by the secretary's desk. She'll have a check for you. And, speaking of seriously, Ms. Maclin, I seriously hope you don't find anything."

BEFORE I LEFT the school, I went back to the cafeteria to speak with Jacey. I asked her to tell me what had happened.

"Mrs. Lever came out as always, lighting up her cigarette and griping about her class."

"And she smoked for a few minutes and then fell over?"

"She went pale and clutched at her heart. Said it was beating too fast. Then she gasped real loud and collapsed. We didn't know what to do except call for the principal."

"By 'we' you mean you and Mrs. Sigmon?"

"Yes, Mrs. Sigmon had just come out."

"To smoke?"

"No, she doesn't smoke. She probably wanted to ask me about making some kind of dough for an art project. Beads, or something. We'd talked about it earlier."

"Did she say anything to Mrs. Lever?"

"Just 'Excuse me,' so she could get by. Mrs. Lever took up more than her share of space. Then Mrs. Lever started carrying on, and when she fell, I didn't know what to do. Mrs. Sigmon told me to call Mister Murphy while she started CPR."

"You called from where?"

"There's a phone just inside the door there. It's usually Mrs. Lever and me this time of day, but it's not like we were big buddies or anything. She never really talked to me. She just complained about her kids."

"Did she ever have trouble breathing, or seem disoriented?"

"Just this one time. Kinda surprising when you figure she smoked whenever she could get the chance."

"So as far as you know, this was the first time she really had some difficulty?"

Jacey nodded. "Mean as she was, I sure didn't like to see her like that, though."

When the dismissal bell rang, I watched from the cafeteria as the students streamed out of their class-rooms and out the doors. Mrs. Lever's class was led by Mrs. Dorman. The children did not seem upset. They laughed and jostled each other as they bounded up the hall. Mrs. Dorman had the same pale strained expres-sion she'd worn when she came to announce the bad news. I wanted to talk to her, but when I got outside, she was surrounded by students, all eagerly trying to get onto busses. I decided to wait until PTA.

I stopped back by the art room. Rachel was push-ing in the chairs. "Quite a day, huh?" she said. "I'll bet you didn't think you'd have this much excitement here at Celosia Elementary."

"I'd like to get my facts straight," I said. "Start from when you left with Jennifer and tell me exactly what happened."

She propped herself on one of the tables. "I helped Jennifer carry the drawings up to Thad's office. On my way back, I remembered I needed to talk to Jacey about making some dough for a bead-making proj-ect I'm starting with my third graders. It would only take a minute, and I knew you had the class in hand— they loved you, by the way. I hope you can come back another day."

"Thanks. I will."

She tucked her hair behind her ears. The little beads on her ear cuff dangled. "Jacey always has a cigarette break around one thirty. Unfortunately, I'd forgotten that Amelia does, too. She almost didn't let me get past her to speak to Jacey. That's when she started gasping and having trouble breathing. She fell, and I told Jacey to call Thad while I tried to revive Amelia. A lot of people on the faculty have CPR training. But by the time Thad came, she'd stopped breathing, and I couldn't do anything else."

"This may sound unkind, but do you think Brenda Mullins could've saved her?"

Rachel wasn't offended. "I don't know. But she wasn't here. I did the best I could."

"I'm sure you did."

"The family's not going to sue me, I hope. I mean, they had to know if Amelia kept smoking like that, something was bound to happen."

"That's why I'm asking these questions."

She looked at her wrist watch. "Well, do you have any more questions? I have to go pick up the girls. Thank goodness they go to Parkland Academy. This would have upset them terribly."

"Your girls don't go to school here?"

"I decided Parkland Academy was better for them."

"No more questions right now."

"Okay. See you tonight?"

"I'll be here," I said.

I WAS A LITTLE surprised to find Fiona Kittering waiting for me at my office door.

"Madeline, did you hear about Amelia Lever?"

I wasn't surprised any more. News traveled very fast in Celosia. "Yes, I happened to be at the school to talk to a class."

"What was it? A heart attack?"

"That's what it looks like."

"Looks like? Are you on a case?" Fiona's eyes went wide. "They think someone murdered her?"

"No, I'm just making sure everyone at the school did all they could."

"I'm sure they did, even though she was a mean old bat—not to speak ill of the dead." I unlocked my door, and Fiona followed me into my office. "But this isn't going to interfere with Nathan's case, is it? He came to you first."

"I won't slight Nathan."

"It's just that he has only one week."

"What do you think the riddle means?"

I thought she'd sit down in the armchair, but she paced in front of my desk. "I've gone over it a million times, and it doesn't make a bit of sense to me. Have you been to see Tori Dewey?"

"Yes, I met her this morning."

"And you got along all right? She didn't throw you out?"

"When's the last time you saw her?"

Fiona stopped pacing. "What do you mean?"

"She's a tiny, shy woman who seems perfectly harmless."

Fiona still didn't answer my question. "She must have really liked you. Did you find out anything?"

"She doesn't mind if I look around. I'm going back to her house tomorrow."

"That's wonderful. I told Nathan you could do it."

"I haven't solved the riddle yet."

"Well, you've certainly made more progress in one day than anyone else."

"I'm taking Jerry with me. He's better at solving riddles."

"She said he could come, too?"

"Yes."

Fiona looked puzzled. I was about to ask her if she'd like to join us when she said, "You two seem very happy."

"We are, thanks."

"I have to say I envy you. Right now, Nathan's putting all his energy into the kids' camp. He's told me as soon as he reaches that goal, he'll have time for our relationship, and I told him I'm behind him one hundred percent." She leaned forward. "You know most people think I'm all business. I am all business. I could really help with that end of the camp. I really want Nathan to succeed."

So finding the answer to the riddle was more important to Fiona than I first thought. "I'm sure we'll find some answers at the chateau."

"That's great, Madeline, thanks."

I expected her to say good-by. Instead, she sat down in the armchair and twisted her hands in her lap. This was the first time I'd seen her in any way unsure. She looked like a terrier confronted with a high wall.

"Was there something else, Fiona?"

"This might be too personal."

"You can ask me anything."

"Personal for me, I mean." She sighed as if she'd made a decision. "Does Nathan seem to show any interest in Tori? Someone told me they were an item years ago. I always thought she had eyes only for Aaron, but apparently, she was a bit of a flirt."

I thought everyone in town of a certain age had gone to high school together, and I couldn't imagine Tori as being flirtatious. "I don't think they're on very good terms, otherwise, he would've gone to the chateau to check the portraits himself, right?"

"I need to be certain. If he still cares for her, I'm not going to waste my time."

"I'm assuming you didn't go to Celosia High School?"

"I moved here about five years ago. Like you, I wanted my own agency in a small town. Maybe I've just heard rumors, but I'd hate to put a lot of effort into a relationship that wasn't going to work."

I hadn't seen any evidence that Nathan was longing for Tori Satterfield, or Fiona, for that matter. He seemed set on winning his fortune and setting up camp. I almost asked Fiona if she wanted to hire me to find out and reconsidered. "Does Nathan know how you feel?"

"As I said, we've been seeing each other for a couple of weeks. It's too soon for me to declare myself. I want to know what I'm getting into."

You're really interested in Nathan's inheritance, I wanted to say. "I think you need to talk to him. Maybe he's ready for a more serious relationship. Maybe he's not. But if he's honest, he'll tell you."

"I hope he'll be honest with me. But you could let me know if he says anything about Tori, couldn't you?"

"It would be better if you asked him," I said. "He's my client."

"That's not much help."

"I'm sorry."

She got up. "Well, thanks, anyway."

I could tell she wanted to say, "Thanks for nothing."

I'D ALREADY PLANNED to meet Jerry at Georgia's after my school visit. His new schedule gave him the rest of the afternoon off.

"Which is very convenient, because I need to go to Parkland and see Warwick," I said.

Jerry gathered a stack of music books from the counter. "Great! I can look for a watch."

"I really need you to run interference."

Jerry grinned. "Doesn't Milton know you're married?"

"That probably won't deter him. And we need to be back here in time for PTA."

He held the door for me and we went out. "PTA? I'll bet that's something you never thought you'd do. What's the occasion? Were you so popular they had to have you back right away?"

"After I talked with Tori Satterfield, I went to Celosia Elementary to speak with Rachel Sigmon's art classes. While I was there, one of the teachers had what looks like a fatal heart attack."

"And you were on the scene! You are the Grim Reaper."

"I want to make sure it was an accident. Mrs. Lever was universally hated and feared."

"Like Mrs. Meerbaum."

We both shuddered. We'd spent a miserable semester with Mrs. Meerbaum for Political Science, a subject neither of us liked. We might have liked it if we'd had a good teacher, but Mrs. Meerbaum was overbearing, sarcastic, and unreasonable.

"Yes, like Mrs. Meerbaum," I said. "The school plans a memorial service tonight during PTA, and I thought I'd scout for suspects. Would you like to come?"

"You know, I don't think I've ever been to a PTA meeting. It might be fun."

"Milton first, then PTA."

"Why don't you just call him?"

"Well, I feel a little guilty. He's been so helpful to me in the past, and I haven't been to see him in a while."

"You're such a pushover."

I unlocked the car and got into the driver's seat. Jerry sat down on the passenger's side and looked through the music books.

"Is that the Christmas cantata?" I asked.

"Yes. *The Glory of Christmas.*"

"Are you planning to play it?"

He leafed through the pages. "I don't know. It's not difficult. I'm not sure I'm ready for the glory of Christmas in September, though."

"Choirs usually start on the Christmas music early, don't they?"

"Well, I wouldn't know, since the last time I was in church, I believe I was wearing a long white dress and crying because my head was wet." He set the book aside. "How was the chateau?"

"Grim and dark. However, Tori Satterfield's really sweet and shy. I don't believe she ever goes out."

"Is she an invalid?"

"No, just shy."

"But she talked to you."

"One artist to another."

"Did she show you her work?"

"Stacks and stacks of scrapbooks, all lovingly decorated. She wanted to be a ballerina and, except for one happy experience, never got the chance."

"Did she know anything about the riddle?"

"No, and there must be a hundred portraits lining the walls."

"Well, if Nathan's so anxious to solve this riddle, why isn't he over there examining all the portraits?"

"I'm not sure. There's something going on or something that used to go on between Nathan and Tori that I can't figure out. But he hired me. And I'm hiring you to come help lift pictures off the walls."

"Okay," he said. "I work cheap."

Milton Warwick met me at the door of his office in Parkland, his broad grin fading when he saw Jerry. But he recovered and beamed like a lighthouse.

"Come in, come in. It's Mr. and Mrs. Fairweather now, isn't it? Congratulations!"

"Thanks," I said.

Milton Warwick's a tall, thin, gangly man with shiny bald head and protuberant eyes. As a scientist, he's interested in everything, and he'd made it clear from the first time we met he was interested in me. I knew he was disappointed I'd married someone else, but his professional curiosity was stronger than his disappointment.

"What can I do for you, Madeline?"

"A teacher at Celosia Elementary died from an apparent heart attack. She was a heavy smoker. She was also wearing a nicotine patch. I want to know if that could've caused a heart attack."

"Well, I'm right in the middle of an experiment.

Give me a few moments. Have a seat, you two. I'll be right back."

Jerry and I sat down in the white plastic chairs Milton keeps for his visitors. Jerry looked through a copy of *Astounding Nonsense,* a magazine published by Milton's science club to debunk myths and questionable scientific research.

"Check this out, Mac. There was an actual paper on the ration of toast crumbs found in butter."

"Our tax dollars at work?"

"An independent study."

"Thank goodness."

"And here's one calculating the number of sled dogs in Alaska. I've always wanted to go to Alaska, but not to count sled dogs."

"Were you thinking of going there any time soon?"

"Sounds pretty cool, doesn't it? How about a second honeymoon?"

"Sure."

"And here's an article on painting." He turned the magazine so I could see. "'Simian Impressionists: An Overview.'"

"Monkey painting. How original."

"That reminds me. How many paintings do you have ready?"

"I'm still trying to decide."

"What about my picture?"

"If you'd sit still long enough, I could finish it."

"What about all those little sketches?"

"They're too small."

"Excuses, excuses."

Milton returned. "So sorry to keep you waiting. Now, to answer your question. You say the victim was wearing a nicotine patch and you want to know if that could have affected her heart. It was a bit foolish of her, but unless she was covered in patches, I doubt it would've caused a heart attack. Do you have access to her medical records? There are a couple of possibilities, but I'd have to know her history."

"Do you know anyone at the Celosia hospital? Can you call in a favor?"

He stroked his little chin. "I might."

"Her name was Amelia Lever."

"Let me see what I can do. I'll call you."

"Thanks, Milton."

"My pleasure, and again, congratulations." He held my hand a little longer than I liked, but I felt sorry for him and didn't pull away. "Jerry, you're a lucky man."

"Yes, I am, thanks."

"You take care of her. Madeline, I'll call as soon as I have any information."

"Okay," Jerry said as we walked back to our car. "I'm looking for a big gold watch with an 'S' on it."

"Any idea where to find one?"

"Foster's Pawnshop."

I might have known Jerry would be familiar with the finer pawnshops of Parkland. Foster's was not what I expected. Instead of a dingy hole in a back alley, the shop was a gleaming modern building with clean floors and an organized array of appliances, musical instruments, and computers. Jerry headed to the back to the glass shelves filled with jewelry. A small gnarled man looked up from the cash register.

"Afternoon, Jerry."

"Bilby, this is my wife, Madeline. Mac, this is Bilby Foster."

I shook hands with the little man, who grinned, showing several gold teeth. "Nice to meet you."

"My pleasure," he said. "Jerry, have you come to buy this lovely lady a nice trinket?"

"I'm looking for a gold pocket watch, specifically one with an 'S' on it."

Foster frowned and pulled out a tray of watches. "Don't think I've got one like that. Have a look. You might see something else you like."

There were plain gold watches, plain silver watches, watches decorated with flowers and vines, watches with pictures of horses or locomotives, and one watch that played a tune when opened.

"I need one with an 'S,'" Jerry said. "Keep an eye out for one, will you?"

"All right. Frankie was asking about you the other day. Wanted to know if you were still interested in what he talked to you about several months ago."

"No, I'm out of that."

Foster looked surprised. "Really? Thought with you wanting a special kind of watch you might be running a little fob off game."

"The watch is for something else."

"Oh." He glanced at me and then winked and made a little zipping motion by his mouth. "Gotcha."

We got back into the car. "Fob off game?" I asked.

"Do you really want to know?" Jerry said.

"Not if you're finished with it."

"I am, I promise."

"You just want to fool Flossie Mae and Sylvie."

"I just want to make them happy. There's a difference. Anywhere else you need to go?"

"I don't think so."

"Why don't we stop by the Weyland Gallery and see where they're going to hang your pictures?"

I had to admit I was curious. "I suppose we could have a look."

The Weyland Gallery was in the Parkland Museum of Art, about twenty minutes from the pawnshop. A young woman at the front desk directed us to the gallery. We walked along quiet halls until we reached the current exhibit, a collection of odd sculptures made of pipes and fuzzy blue circles mounted on twisted coat hangers.

"If this were a contest, I think you'd win," Jerry said.

A severe-looking woman in black, her silver hair skinned back in a tight bun, overheard him and turned to scowl.

"This is a fine example of Late Twentieth Century mood pieces. The artist is one of our brightest young people working in three dimensions."

"Of course," I said. "It's very dynamic."

This seemed to appease her. "Good choice of words." She held out a thin hand. "I'm Letticia Booth, curator of the Weyland Gallery."

Oh, great. One woman I do not want to offend. "I'm Madeline Maclin Fairweather, and this is my husband, Jerry."

"Fairweather, Fairweather, why do I know that name?"

"I'm entering your New Artists Show."

Her smile made her look more approachable. "Oh, yes. Your 'Blue Moon Garden' is quite a nice piece of modern impressionism. I'm looking forward to seeing more of your work."

"Thank you. We hadn't been in the Weyland Gallery and thought we'd look around."

She gestured toward a wall filled with paintings. "Allow me."

We followed Letticia Booth as she went from room to room, giving us a brief overview of the collection.

"Now here we have some neo-classical nonstructured landscapes, and here are the works of Joachim Handlemeyer, a protégé of Van Dyke, who never got the recognition he deserved. And here are our French Impressionists. I believe you'll be interested in those."

As I looked at the beautiful paintings, I thought, yes, that's the way to suggest the light on leaves. That's the way to show movement in the grass. I'd almost forgotten how inspiring the classic works could be. I knew immediately how I could improve my landscapes. I wanted more than ever to be a part of this.

"And in the next room we have some lovely examples of trompe-l'oeil," Letticia Booth said. "We're especially proud of the Marquesa still life." She chatted on until we were back to the pipes and circles.

"Thank you so much," I said.

"My pleasure. Am I to understand that you work full-time as an artist?"

"Actually, I have my own agency in Celosia, Madeline Maclin Investigations."

"I see. And what sort of things do you investigate?"

"Missing persons, lost objects, and I help with murder investigations."

Letticia Booth looked taken aback. "Really? But you want a career in art, as well?"

Did I want a career in art as well as a career as a private investigator? Why not? Why couldn't I have both? I gave Jerry a smile. "Yes," I said, and for the first time, I meant it.

"Well, that's quite interesting." She wore a watch on a long silver chain. She glanced at it. "I have an opening in my schedule. Come to my office. I'd like to hear more about this."

Letticia Booth's office was a vast spacious room decorated in plum and gray with framed black and white photographs of flowers on the walls. Spaced in front of the window were three short Greek columns, each one with a sculpture or vase or piece of modern art placed on top. The view from the window showed a garden with Japanese maples just beginning to turn red.

"Please have a seat," she said. "May I offer you some tea?"

"No, thank you," I said. The plum-colored chairs in front of her desk were oddly shaped but very comfortable.

"I really enjoy getting to know our new artists. Tell me how you became involved with investigating crimes."

"I used to work at an agency here in Parkland, but I decided to leave and start an agency of my own." I explained that while Jerry and I were in Celosia to check on a house he'd inherited, I was hired to investigate sabotage at the Miss Celosia Pageant, and in the course of that investigation, found one of the contestants dead backstage.

"I was able to find out who killed her. And then a director wanted to use the house for his horror movie. Someone poisoned him, and I discovered his murderer, as well."

"Very interesting. Do you feel your talents are put to their best use on murder investigations?"

"I don't always have cases like that. I like finding lost articles, missing relatives, family heirlooms." When I'm not being challenged by murder mysteries, I wanted to add.

"If your art work were to become popular, would you have the time to spend on it?"

"Fortunately, the murder cases are few."

"Well, you're a very attractive young woman. Some of the artists I've met, quite frankly, look as though they've been sleeping in Dumpsters. This could be a good story for the museum, a good way for the show to get more positive publicity. I'd like you to meet our liaison to the *Parkland Herald*."

For a horrible moment, I thought she was going to say, "Chance Baseford," the critic who'd shredded my first exhibit. But she said, "Valerie Banner. May I call her and set up an interview?"

A favorable showing at the gallery and a positive interview in the paper would go a long way toward improving my reputation as an artist. "Yes, thank you," I said.

"I believe we have your contact information. I'll have her call you."

As we left the museum, Jerry took my arm in his. "I feel a Twenty-First Century mood coming on," he said.

"A good mood?"

"Oh, yes. You accomplished quite a lot in that short visit. If Valerie Banner writes a decent story, you might even get more cases."

"Just so she doesn't write something like, 'Murder is an Art,' or 'A Brush With Death.'"

"Or 'Color Me Dead.'"

WE ENTERTAINED OURSELVES with more headlines as we drove back to Celosia and home.

Home. Yes, when I thought of the house, I thought of it as home, a home slowly emerging from years of neglect to become a beautiful, inviting place, set in a field of waving grass and wildflowers, and surrounded by ancient oak trees. Before moving here, I'd lived in a small apartment in Parkland, and before that, Bill and I had a large, ugly, split-level house. The only other home I'd had was my mother's house with its cold black and white décor and uncomfortable furniture. I never wanted to go back to any of those places.

I know Jerry loves the house, I thought, but this house means something to me, too. I love our blue living room. I love our kitchen at the back with the old fashioned table and chairs. I love my upstairs studio with its wonderful light and the front porch where Jerry and I watch the sunsets.

The white van parked under one of the trees meant Nell Brenner, our handywoman, was here. While Jerry went into the kitchen in search of a snack, I found Nell upstairs replacing the front of a new air conditioning unit.

"Heard there was a little commotion over at the school," she said.

It no longer startles me that Nell knows everything that happens in town, sometimes before it happens. "Amelia Lever had a heart attack."

Nell wiped her large hands on her paint splattered overalls. "Passed on, did she?"

"Yes, and I'm not so sure it was of natural causes."

She reached into her toolbox for her screwdriver.

She gave me a glance from her small shrewd blue eyes. "You on the case?"

"Not exactly."

She tightened the screws that held on the front panel. "Well, I can tell you that Amelia Lever was a hateful woman, and I'm a little surprised someone hasn't killed her before now."

"Hateful in general, or did something make her hateful?"

"Can't figure it. She married George Lever, had the two boys, taught school forever. Must have been something in her childhood. Why are you interested?"

Why was I interested? Well, for one thing, the idea of a murder happening at Austin and Denisha's elementary school made me very uncomfortable. "She was wearing a nicotine patch and smoking at the same time."

"Probably just forgot—or do you think somebody saw her light up and smacked a patch on her?" Nell chuckled. "I'd like to see the man or woman brave enough to smack Amelia Lever."

"Well, then, what can you tell me about Victoria Satterfield?"

Nell straightened and turned on the unit. Cool air blew the wisps of blond hair sticking out from under her baseball cap. "Oh, yeah, Tori Dewey. Nice girl. Kinda shy."

"She's built herself a fort out of scrapbooks and old newspapers."

"That husband of hers was no good. She probably needed some kind of protection. Took to you, did she?"

"We have art in common."

"Poor girl didn't have much of anything. Not a bad

dancer as I hear it. She deserved a little bit of the spotlight. Too bad Aaron Satterfield didn't feel the same way."

"Then why did he marry her?"

She readjusted the fan level to turn back the arctic blast. "Basically to spite his family. They'd picked out some rich girl from up north. He wasn't going to do what they said. A stubborn boy, real arrogant."

"What can you tell me about Nathan Fenton?"

"Nathan Fenton's all right. He and Fiona Kittering oughta make a good couple. Both of them dull as dirt."

"What about this Camp Lakenwood?"

Nell's eyes gleamed the same way Nathan's had gleamed when he talked about the camp. "I have some real happy memories about that place. Went there every summer. Learned all kinds of crafts. Fixed everything I could get my hands on."

I imagined a smaller version of Nell chopping down trees and building log cabins.

"So this camp idea is legitimate?"

"If he wants to fix it up, I say more power to him."

"Does it need a lot of repair?"

"Well, it hasn't been open for several years now. I'd say it would take some serious money to set it right."

"Fiona tells me Fenton's Uncle Elijah was not nice to know."

"He was a right ornery old cuss." She picked up her toolbox and pulled her hat firmly down. "So now you tell me how things are with you and junior. He miss that wild life of his?"

"I don't think so."

"Still holds them séances, doesn't he?"

"Just for Mrs. Snyder and Sylvie."

"Any more of his idiot friends come to visit?"

"You'd know it if they were here."

Her little eyes twinkled. "Why, yes, I would. Cool enough for you?"

"Yes, it feels great."

She reached over and turned the air conditioner down. "Oughta work fine now."

Jerry was sitting on the front porch eating out of a large bag of Cheetos. Nell gave him a wave as she went down the porch steps to her van. In a few minutes, the van chugged down the driveway.

"Where are the kids?" I asked.

"I don't know. They're usually here by now. It wasn't their teacher who died, was it?"

"No, they're in Mrs. Forrest's class."

He tipped the bag my way. I shook my head. He took another handful. "So what's your plan?"

"I'm going to talk to as many teachers as I can tonight. Maybe I can have a look in Amelia's classroom." I gazed across the fields that surrounded our house. Crickets were cheeping. The September sun was golden on the tall grass and yellow wildflowers. Some milkweed tufts had caught in a spider web. I'd lived all my young life in hotel rooms and dance studios and practice rooms, in auditoriums, ball rooms, and in the dark backstages of who knows how many theaters, while all this time, nature was going on. I'd almost missed it.

Since Jerry's younger brother, Tucker, is a gardener, Jerry knows the names of almost all the plants. He'd pointed out the larkspur and butterfly bushes around the porch, the altheas and hydrangeas. I always felt so happy sitting out here on the porch with him as we sur-

veyed our somewhat unkempt kingdom. I hoped Jerry
felt the same way.

"What are you thinking about?" he asked.

"Just how beautiful all this is."

"So you don't miss the big city?"

"Not at all. Do you?"

He crunched a few more Cheetos before he answered. "Sometimes."

I was glad for the opening. "I don't want you to
think you're stuck here."

"I wouldn't call it stuck. I like it here."

I sat down on the porch rail. "I was also thinking
about how much I love this house."

"Told you it would grow on you."

"And I love this town—if people would stop kill-
ing each other."

"Unfortunately, that happens everywhere."

Inside the house, I heard the jingling tune of my cell
phone. "I hope that's not another one."

I went into the living room and dug my phone out
of my pocketbook. When I checked the caller ID I
almost didn't answer. Then I took a deep breath and
said, "Hello?"

"Hello, Madeline," my mother said.

Might as well be cheerful. "Oh, hi, Mom, how are
you?"

"You were in Parkland today and didn't call? You
could've come by the house. Your cousins were here
from Ohio. I'm sure they would've loved to have seen
you. And they were so sorry they didn't know about your
wedding. I'm sure they would've loved to have come."

In the past, these layers of guilt would have smoth-
ered me. However, I'm on to my mother's tricks. Plus I
knew my cousins didn't care a thing about seeing me or

coming to my wedding. Like my mother, they'd given up on me when I renounced my pageant ways. "It was a business trip. I had just a few hours."

"Business? Do you mean that little agency of yours?" I could imagine her holding the phone with one hand while she inspected her fingernails. I was sure she had on an immaculately tailored suit, most likely in black and white, her favorite non-colors. "Don't tell me you're finding enough work in Celosia."

"I'm working on two cases right now."

"Is Jerry working? What's he doing?"

Putting the finishing touches on what I hope will be his last scam. "He's still at the bookstore."

"Will he not take any of that money he's entitled to?"

"We're getting along fine, Mom."

"Claudia Mayfield said she saw you at the Weyland Gallery. Whatever were you doing there?"

My mother had always seen my art work as a foolish past time. When my first exhibit was panned, she saw this as proof I had no artistic talent. I took a moment to fashion just the right answer. "The Weyland asked to show some of my work as part of their New Artists Series."

Silence.

"You'll be able to see it next week. I'll have three paintings in the show."

More silence.

"One of the paintings they really like is 'Blue Moon Garden.' You may remember that one."

"Well," she said. "Well, that's very nice, Madeline. Congratulations."

It had taken a lot for her to say that. "Thank you. I hope you'll come to the show."

"I'd like that. The Weyland is the finest gallery in town, you know. That's quite an accomplishment."

I could hear her brain whirring as it readjusted its world view. Not my daughter, the Pageant Queen, or Ace Detective, but my daughter, the Upcoming Artist. She could use this to keep turning in her social circle.

"Will there be some sort of reception?"

"I'll make sure you get all the details," I said. "I'd like for you to come." If she couldn't be the mother I wanted, at least I wanted her as a friend. If having a daughter to brag about was the only way she could justify being a mother, then I was glad I'd done something right.

"This is good news, Madeline. I'll see you at the gallery."

"Thanks," I said. I hung up and went back to the porch. "That was Mother. Hang on to the railing because I'm about to tell you something shocking. She's happy about the art show."

Jerry grinned. "About time she was happy about something."

"She saw us in Parkland. Her spies are everywhere."

"Maybe we should visit her next time we're in town."

"Let's start with the art show. Give her time to adjust."

"Okay."

"And speaking of adjusting, you sure you don't miss your wandering days?"

"Not really."

"Is there enough in Celosia to keep you busy?"

He set the bag aside. "What's all this about?"

"I just don't want you to be bored."

"Bored? Well, let's see. I have my Bufo collection, my piano, my work at the bookstore, and the prospect of a hot night at the Celosia Elementary PTA watching ace investigator, Madeline Maclin Fairweather, in action. How could I be bored?"

"Seriously, Jerry. We really should have discussed this more before we got married."

"What's to discuss? We're together, and that's all that matters to me."

I was surprised by the tears that stung my eyes. I gave Jerry a long hug so he wouldn't see the tears, and I could get myself under control.

"What's up?" he asked. "Look, if this gallery thing and your mom is going to be too much stress—"

"No, it's fine." It really was fine. Usually a call from my mother left me feeling depressed and heavy, but I felt light, as if I'd been carrying a weight I didn't know I had. "Let's go pick out the perfect tie for you to wear tonight."

"Would that be upstairs in our bedroom?"

"Yes." I gave him a kiss. "Right now."

THREE

JERRY DECIDED HIS green tie with the monkeys and bananas was appropriate for a school meeting. I wore a more conservative black skirt and red blouse. I had a chance to speak to several teachers before the meeting. All of them were sorry such an incident had happened during the school day, but not one expressed any deep regret that Amelia Lever had died.

During the business part of the PTA meeting, Jerry peeled a Bufo sticker from the back of the chair in front of me. The sticker showed Bufo in a heroic pose, his Sword of Thunder held aloft, his Shield of Justice deflecting the harmful rays of his enemies' Battle Bolts. I showed the sticker to Rachel, who was sitting on my right. She shook her head.

"Those things are everywhere."

Thad Murphy came on stage. He introduced the chorus members who sang a song about "Living Your Dreams" in honor of Mrs. Lever. I thought Mrs. Lever wasn't living anything at this point. Murphy gave a brief talk about Amelia's accomplishments at Celosia Elementary and then introduced her two grown sons, Kevin and Marshall Lever.

Amelia's sons thanked Thad and the PTA for honoring their mother. The two men looked like twins. They had unfashionable Prince Valiant haircuts and ugly flannel shirts, but their trousers and shoes looked expensive. They were shy and sad-faced, like two dachs-hunds that had wandered away from their yard.

Thad Murphy had some closing remarks. "As for Mrs. Lever's class, we're pleased to announce that Miss Norma Olsen will be coming in tomorrow to take over the class. I hope all of you will make Miss Olsen feel welcome during this difficult time."

After the meeting, Jerry and I offered our condolences to Kevin and Marshall Lever. Rachel said, "I'm so very sorry. I know you'll miss your mother very much."

"Thank you," Kevin Lever said. "It was really nice of you folks to have this for her."

"Is her funeral tomorrow? I'd like to come."

He looked at his brother. "We don't belong to a church. We're having Mother cremated as soon as possible."

Marshall Lever said, "Not to sound too harsh, but we didn't get along with Mother that well. When we heard you folks were going to do this tonight, we thought being here was the least we could do."

Jerry gave me a look. I knew what he was thinking. You have to be desperate or damned uncaring to come hear a few words about your dead mother at an elementary school PTA meeting. Or maybe "relieved" was the word I was looking for. The Lever boys showed no signs of grief.

"It's too bad your mother forgot she was wearing a nicotine patch," I said.

The brothers shared another unreadable glance. "Yes," Kevin said. "It's not like her to forget anything."

"Could something have happened to distract her?"

"Not at school," Marshall said. "She was single-minded about her work."

"She was single-minded about everything," Kevin said. "Did she have any friends here? Don't worry. I'll be very surprised if you say yes."

I could tell Rachel was choosing her words carefully. "She was hard to get close to."

"Did the children like her?"

"They respected her. Ronald Brown, especially."

Thad Murphy came over, and soon the Levers were surrounded by other parents and teachers. Rachel, Jerry, and I stepped away.

Rachel introduced me to other members of the faculty. Everyone said pretty much the same thing. Amelia Lever was a good teacher, but a difficult person. She wasn't a joiner, she was very strict with her students, and she should've retired years ago.

"Why didn't she, then?" I asked Rachel.

"Who knows?"

"Maybe she needed the money," Jerry said.

"And if she was too strict with her students, why wasn't she let go?"

"Oh, her students always scored very high on the end of grade tests," Rachel said. "That's extremely important to the school. I'm sure if her kids had done poorly, Thad wouldn't have put up with her as long as he did. Could you excuse me? I need to get to my classroom. The parents will be coming in to have a look at their kids' artwork."

"We'll see you later," I said. "We're going to walk around. Where's Mrs. Lever's classroom?"

"The end of the first hall."

From the art room, Jerry and I walked the short

distance to the cafeteria. No chance of finding any incriminating footprints. The steps down to the cafeteria and the floors were scrubbed and shiny.

"Let's go out to the loading dock first," I said. "I may have overlooked something."

The dock was empty and clean. "No clues here," Jerry said.

"Let's check around the trash cans."

We went down the short flight of metal steps to the driveway. The area around the trash cans was clean. The trash cans were empty.

"I'm glad to know our public schools are this tidy," Jerry said. "But it plays hell with finding clues."

There was a narrow strip of grass between the dock and some sort of large generator or air conditioning unit. I bent down and searched through the grass, finding a dime, a marble, an eraser, plastic wrap from a cigarette pack, and a small piece of clear plastic.

I held it up. "Any idea what this is?"

Jerry took it. "Looks like the top part of a pen. I don't know." He handed it back to me. "Could be a piece of a kid's toy."

"I'll take all these things, too."

We went back inside and walked down the fourth grade hall. Teachers stood at their classroom doorways, greeting parents. Mrs. Dorman stood at the door to Mrs. Lever's classroom.

"Mrs. Dorman, could we come have a look around?" I asked.

She frowned at me. "This is not the time. I'm very busy talking with parents."

"I don't need to ask you any questions right now. I'd just like to see Mrs. Lever's classroom."

She glared at me and lowered her voice. "Come back tomorrow afternoon when no one is here. There's no reason to upset the children."

From what I could see, the children were eagerly showing their parents their schoolwork and projects. "It doesn't look like anyone's upset."

"Of course not! The children haven't grasped the seriousness of this matter, and their parents are trying to act as if everything is normal. Please go away. You can look all you like tomorrow."

I certainly didn't want to make a scene. "I'll see you tomorrow, then."

"Well, that's an ornery old turtle," Jerry said as we walked back up the hall.

"I can't fault her for trying to keep things normal."

"Normal? Try invisible."

"Excuse me." A tall man in a blue track suit stopped us. With him was a sturdy-looking dark-haired boy. I recognized the boy as the same student who had asked me about whacking Bernice King with the umbrella. "I couldn't help but overhear you talking with Mrs. Dorman. I'm Oscar Brown, and this is my son, Ronald. Do you have a child in the class?"

"No," I said. "I'm Madeline Maclin Fairweather, and this is my husband, Jerry." I didn't want to mention the possibility of foul play in front of Ronald. "We're just visiting the school."

We all shook hands, and Oscar Brown said, "Well, we're not all heartless around here. Ronald liked Mrs. Lever, and I appreciated her tough approach to teaching. We were very sorry to hear about her, but, unfortunately, she was a heavy smoker. Ronald and I had talked about that."

"Yeah," Ronald said. "She wheezed all the time."

"Did she ever try to quit?"

"She was trying those patch things."

"Too little too late," Oscar Brown said. "I understand she'd had health problems for years."

"And now we're going to have that sappy Ms. Olsen," Ronald said.

His father frowned. "Ronald, I told you not to make any more comments like that about your new teacher."

"But, Dad, she's like a big ball of goo."

I could tell Mr. Brown was trying to keep a straight face. "You still need to respect her. You might learn something from her."

"Yeah, how to make daisy chains and sing 'Kumbaya.'"

Oscar Brown looked at us apologetically and shrugged. "It's going to be an adjustment. Come on, Ron, you wanted me to meet your P.E. teacher. Nice to have met you folks."

We continued up the hall. "Well, it's good to know Amelia had at least one fan," Jerry said.

"And it's beginning to look more and more like she died from a heart attack."

"If she had a heart," said a voice.

We'd reached the last classroom on the hall. A young woman grinned at us. "Sorry. Had to say it."

"Did you have a problem with Mrs. Lever?"

"Certainly did. A little matter of an art and music grant."

"The same one Mrs. Sigmon applied for?"

The young woman's expression hardened. "That was the most blatant piece of sabotage I've ever seen. Lever deliberately screwed up the part she was supposed to write until it was too late to make the deadline."

"And why would she do that?"

"She thought the arts were useless. She never wanted to send her kids to art, or to music, for that matter. She said art and music were just a waste of time."

A group of parents approached, and the young woman's expression returned to bright cheerfulness. "Hello! Welcome to the music room!"

"Yup, just one devoted fan," Jerry said as we walked away.

When we came back to the art room, Rachel was talking to an overweight young woman with long curly brown hair and stiff bangs.

"I can't tell you how excited I am to finally get this job," she was saying. "Not that I'm rejoicing over her death, you understand, but things worked out really well for me."

"Madeline, this is Norma Olsen," Rachel said. "She'll be taking over Amelia's class."

I shook Ms. Olsen's hand. "Nice to meet you."

Norma Olsen had a wide beaming smile that probably never dimmed. "Thanks. This will be my first class ever. I'm really excited."

I wondered if anyone else had been considered for the job. "I'm not sure how it works in a school. Were you next in line?"

"Sort of. I'd been promised the job last summer, and then Amelia came back for another year. I was really furious, and then I thought, well, that's just another example of how this school system operates. Now I have to take back all the ugly things I said about Thad and the school board."

"Everyone was expecting Mrs. Lever to retire?"

"She should've retired years ago. She wasn't just burnt out. She was nothing but ashes."

She is now, I thought. Or soon will be.

"Well, I've got tons to do to get ready for tomorrow. See you tomorrow, Rachel!"

When Norma Olsen had gone down the hall, Rachel said, "Did you find out anything?"

"No, but I'm coming back tomorrow after school to talk with Mrs. Dorman."

"Would I sound completely hard-hearted if I asked you to come a little earlier and continue your talk with my art classes?"

"No, that's fine." I didn't mind an excuse to be at the school.

"Great! See you tomorrow, then."

Jerry and I had just left the art room when Austin and Denisha rushed up to us.

"Madeline, what do you think? Are you going to solve the mystery? She was murdered, right? Who do you think did it?"

"Hold on," I said. "We don't know for sure what happened to Mrs. Lever."

Denisha clapped her hands. "In our own school! This is so neat. It was lucky you were here."

Denisha's aunt, Averall Mercer, and Austin's mother, Samantha Terrell, came up. Both were shaking their heads.

"Austin, for heaven's sake, calm down," Samantha said.

Averall made a "tsking" sound with her tongue. "Denisha Simpson, you control yourself. Stop jumping on Madeline like you haven't got good sense."

Austin was still bouncing. "But it's a murder, Mom, and Madeline's a detective."

"It was an accident," Samantha said.

"Then why is Madeline at PTA?"

"I'm just making sure I have all the information," I said. "Right now, it does look like an accident."

"But nobody liked her," Denisha said. "I was so glad I got Mrs. Forrest instead of her."

Averall shushed her niece. "That doesn't mean someone killed her. There are lots of unlikable people walking around. Mrs. Lever shouldn't have been smoking." She steered Denisha toward the door. "Time to go home. Tomorrow's another school day."

Austin tugged on his mother's arm. "They oughta close school on account of Mrs. Lever being dead. It could be a national day of mourning."

"It could be, but it's not going to be," she said. "Come on. You've got some homework to finish."

"Awww."

As Jerry and I went out, we saw Kevin and Marshall Lever standing just outside the front door of the school, still accepting condolences from parents and teachers.

Jerry snapped his fingers. "Now I know where I've seen those guys before."

"Amelia's sons?"

"Yes, the winners of the Moe Howard look-alike contest. One of them was in the store the other day with a woman who must have been Amelia."

"What did they buy?"

Jerry tried to look innocent and failed. "Well, I never eavesdrop on my customers' conversations."

"I'm sure that never happens."

"But they were arguing so loudly, everyone in

the store heard them. I should say she was arguing.
The poor guy was trying to get in a word or two. It
had something to do with a wedding. I gathered she
wasn't too happy about his choice of a bride. She said,
'No one in the Lever family has ever married without
permission.' Then the man said something about wanting 'Silver Archer Number Six,' and she told him he
was an idiot."

"Anything else?"

Jerry shook his head. "A lot of times couples argue
over the merits of having a comic collection. I try to
keep out if it."

"Did he buy the comic?"

"No, she made him leave without buying anything."

"So she didn't approve of his bride to be. A lot of
mothers don't."

"The Lever brothers look old enough to make their
own decisions."

"They don't seem very grief-stricken, but they said
they weren't close to their mother. I'm not really close
to mine."

"But would you give her a Deadly Cigarette of
Doom?"

"That sounds like something Bufo might do, not
me. I'll visit the Lever brothers tomorrow after I've
had a word with Mrs. Dorman."

"And Tori Satterfield. I can't wait to see Castle
Groundhog."

"She's very shy," I said. "She spends her time creating scrapbooks of different ballets."

"So she's not really an artist?"

"Not in the ordinary sense. And speaking of art, I'd
like to get home and do some work."

Back in my studio, I got so involved with the field landscape, I couldn't believe it was almost midnight when Jerry came in to check on my progress.

He stood in front of his portrait, chin in hand. "Well, the picture of me can hardly be improved upon. Have you decided on a third?"

I'd spent the last thirty minutes agonizing between rust and gold on the leaves. "I don't know. I'd like all three pictures to work together, but there isn't a common theme."

"Leave mine out and do a third abstract landscape."

"I'm not sure there's time. It's already Tuesday morning."

"Come on to bed. You'll have a better idea in the morning."

"I hope so," I said.

He grinned. "Meanwhile, I have some ideas."

"I'll just bet you do."

I SET MY ALARM CLOCK for seven and managed to get up when it rang. I started another abstract and worked in my studio until about eight, when Jerry called up the stairs that breakfast was ready. He'd fixed bacon and eggs. I sat down to eat when the phone rang. He answered it and then handed it to me.

"It's Valerie Banner."

Valerie Banner sounded as if she were about sixteen years old. "Mrs. Fairweather? I'm Valerie Banner, reporter for the *Parkland Herald*. How are you this morning?"

"Fine, thanks."

"I'd like to set up a time when we could meet so I

could interview you for the paper. If we could do it today, I'd have the article ready for the Sunday edition."

"We can do it right now."

"Oh, but I'd like to get a photo. What's your schedule like today? I could come to Celosia if that's easier for you."

Besides going to Tori's, I had my return appointment with Rachel's art classes, and many more people to talk to. "Ms. Banner, I have limited time today."

"Could I meet you for lunch somewhere, then?"

"I'll probably be at Deely's Burger World, if you're familiar with it."

"I'll say! I love their cheeseburgers. I'll meet you there around eleven thirty, if that's okay. I won't take but about twenty minutes."

I started to describe myself so we could find each other, but she interrupted.

"Oh, I know what you look like. See you later."

I hung up. "She's going to meet me at Deely's."

Jerry put more bacon on my plate. "Did she say how you could recognize her? She sounded like a teenager."

"No, but she said she knows what I look like. I hope she's not a pageant groupie. I really don't want her story to have any sort of beauty queen angle."

"I don't think Valerie was alive when you were Queen of Parkland."

I reached over to smack his shoulder. "Thanks a lot."

"You'll have to ask her if she's got a relative working in the newspaper business. Seems to me I've heard the name Banner before." The phone rang again, and he answered it. "Good morning. Oh, hi, Sylvie. Any luck?" He listened for a few moments and then said, "What, this morning? Sure, come on. Yeah, I'll be here, no problem. Okay, see you after a while." He hung up. "Flossie Mae and Sylvie didn't find the watch behind the door."

"I'm shocked."

"Sylvie seems to think a quick trip to the spirit world is in order."

"So they're coming over right now?"

"Just Sylvie. Flossie Mae has a hair appointment." He put more eggs on his plate and sat down at the table.

I took a sip of coffee. "Now would be the perfect time to come clean."

"We'll see what the spirits have to say."

"Will the spirits be done by the time we're expected at the chateau?"

"I'm sure they will."

"Jerry, just tell her there's no gold watch. It'll save everybody a lot of trouble."

I thought I had him convinced until Sylvie arrived. "Oh, gosh, I've interrupted your breakfast," she said.

"Not at all," Jerry said. "Come sit down and have some coffee. I can fix more bacon and eggs, if you like."

"No, thanks." She pushed back her untidy long brown hair. "I know this is sort of sudden, but I really need to know the location of the watch."

I gave Jerry a warning glare, which he ignored. "I'll be glad to help. Give me a few minutes to set up."

He went into the front parlor. "Sylvie," I said, "you shouldn't rely on what Jerry tells you. This isn't real, you know. It's more like entertainment."

Her eyes were wide. "Oh, it's very real to me. I know he has a link to the other side. You can't fake these things."

Okay. Looked like the harder I protested, the more she was going to believe. "I don't want you to be disappointed if he can't find this watch."

"Well, really it's up to me and Aunt Flossie to find it. We just have to interpret the clues he gives us."

"What exactly will you do with it if you find it?"

She looked at me as if I'd asked what will you do with the Holy Grail? "Put it in a place of honor, of course. Treasure it. Hand it down to my children and tell them the story of how it was found, how Aunt Marge and Aunt Marie fought so bitterly in life but were transformed by the healing power of the light of eternity."

I did not have an answer for this.

"Okay, Sylvie," Jerry called from the parlor. "Show time."

I followed Sylvie as she hurried to the parlor. She sat down at the table where a fat candle glowed. Jerry took her hand. "I'm not sure what kind of response we'll get, Sylvie. It's a little harder in the daytime, you know."

She nodded. "I'm just so grateful you're willing to do this."

Did Jerry look just the teensiest bit guilty at her blinding faith in his non-existent ability to speak to the dead? I hoped so.

"Okay, here we go."

He closed his eyes and went through his usual array of noises. Sylvie watched him anxiously. Then he jerked in his chair and began to speak in a higher voice.

"What is it, my child?"

Sylvie had to take a breath. "Is it Aunt Marge or Aunt Marie?"

"Aunt Marge."

"It's about the watch, Aunt Marge. Aunt Flossie and I still haven't been able to find it. We've looked behind every door we could find. We even looked on the porch Uncle Ray closed off. I was hoping you could give me a better idea where it is. We don't have enough information."

Jerry hummed tunelessly for a few minutes and then said, "Is the watch that important to you, Sylvie?"

She looked taken aback. "Yes, it is. It's very important."

"Wouldn't something else do, say, a fond memory of your Aunt Marge?"

"But I don't have any fond memories of you, or of Aunt Marie. You were always fighting. The watch would be a symbol of your newfound friendship in heaven."

Jerry gulped. I couldn't tell if this was part of his act or his realization he was losing his grip on the situation. "But we are very happy in heaven, dear. Don't you believe me?"

"Yes, but something I could hold and pass along to my children would be so much better. And you did promise."

Another gulp. "I'll see what I can do. I—I must leave you now. The light. I must return to the light." Jerry gave a realistic gasp and came out of his so-called trance. "Did one of them come through? What did she say?"

Sylvie looked pleased. "She's going to see what she can do. Thank you, Jerry."

She started to get out her wallet. "No, that's okay," he said. "You can pay me later."

"Thanks."

After she'd gone, I looked at him. "Nice try."

He gave me a wry grin. "That's what happens when you try to reach the spirits in the morning."

"You might be more helpful at Tori's."

WHEN TORI MET US at the door of the chateau and saw Jerry, she took a step back and wrapped her thin arms tightly around herself.

I wasn't sure what had alarmed her. "Tori, this is my husband, Jerry."

Jerry kept his distance and smiled. "Mrs. Satterfield, I'm Jerry Fairweather. Mac's brought me along for the heavy lifting."

I don't know if it was his calm voice or his smile or the joke about heavy lifting, but Tori relaxed slightly. Her voice faltered. "Welcome to my home."

He stayed where he was, still smiling. "It's beautiful. I've never been in a castle before."

"It's not exactly a castle."

"Mac tells me you've created some beautiful scrapbooks."

She brightened. "Did she tell you I once danced the part of Clara in *The Nutcracker?*"

"I can certainly see that, Mrs. Satterfield."

"Please call me Tori." She hesitated another minute. "Come in."

Once she no longer perceived him as a threat, it didn't take long for Tori to respond to Jerry's lively manner. He listened patiently as she explained each clipping on the pages of her latest scrapbook, made admiring comments, and occasionally gave me a wide-eyed glance as if to say, can you believe this?

Tori finally came to the end of the book. "And what do you do, Jerry?"

"I work at Georgia's Books. Sometimes I do magic tricks."

"Do you really?"

"Sure. Watch this." He took a quarter out of his pocket and made it disappear.

Tori was delighted. "How do you do that?"

"It's not hard. It just takes a lot of practice. I could teach you."

"I'd like that."

"But you have to tell me one thing."

"All right," she said.

"Why is your castle named after a groundhog?"

She made a face. "Elijah Fenton thought 'marmot' was the French word for 'marvelous,' and no one had the courage to correct him."

I thought "Marmot" was an appropriate name for someone who basically lived in a burrow.

"Mac, you ought to create a coat of arms for the castle: two rodents rampant on a field of gold."

To my amazement, Tori gave a little giggle. "I suppose I could," I said.

Tori's gaze strayed back to the piles of paper. "Madeline, have you and Jerry been to the ballet lately?"

"I've been several times, but Jerry prefers the opera."

She looked impressed. "I don't believe I've ever been to a real opera. I've seen some on TV." She glanced at the piles of trimmings on the table. I could almost see her mind formulating a new collection. "Do you have anything you could spare for my book? A program or a ticket stub? Anything?"

"I might have a few things," Jerry said. "I'll see what I can find."

She clasped her fragile hands together. "That would be wonderful. Now, let's go find the answer to that riddle."

We started in the long hall that led from Tori's hideout to the dining room. Jerry looked up at the frowning face in the first portrait.

"Who's this?"

"Elijah's sister, Eulalie Fenton."

"She looks fierce."

"She was."

"And this guy?"

"Ellis Fenton, Nathan's father."

"Equally grim." Jerry lifted the picture from its hook and turned it around. Nothing. We moved on to the next relative.

"Oh, this is nice," Jerry said. "He's got a little dog."

"That's Elijah's grandfather, Hobarth, with Ticky."

"Ticky? Was he full of ticks?"

Tori laughed. "No, no. I think he was ticklish."

There was nothing behind Hobarth and Ticky. There was nothing behind second cousin Elizabeth or great-aunt Aubergine. As we searched, Tori became more animated.

We worked our way down one side of the hall and then took a break.

Tori dusted her hands. "Well, this is discouraging, but as you can see, there's lots more."

I looked at my watch. It was almost eleven. "I've got to meet someone, Tori. Can we come back later?"

"Yes, of course. You may come back any time."

"How about tomorrow morning?"

"I look forward to it." She showed us to the door, gave a little wave, and hurried back to her nest.

Jerry shook his head. "Man, that's pathetic. We've got to get her out of there."

"Only if she wants to, Jerry. I think she's borderline agoraphobic."

"All that newspaper and dust. It's like being in a tomb. I need a drink."

"Coke and a cheeseburger at Deely's?"

"That oughta do it."

WE GOT TO DEELY'S well before the lunch crowd and found a booth next to the front windows.

"I can be on the lookout for our junior reporter," I said.

After ordering, Jerry said, "If you want to know about Elijah Fenton, you can always ask The Geezer Club. They probably knew him."

"The Geezer Club" was Jerry's name for the three elderly men who met every morning at a corner table of the restaurant to eat ham biscuits, drink coffee, and sound off on everything that didn't suit them about Celosia and the world at large. They were still at their favorite spot. The men looked identical in their overalls and baseball caps, but I knew one man was Horace Stanley, one of Nell's great-uncles.

I strolled up to them. "Good morning, gentlemen."

Mister Stanley tipped his baseball cap. One man gave me a nod. The other brushed crumbs off the front of his shirt.

"Mornin,' Mrs. Fairweather," Horace said. He was a distinguished looking man with a large moustache.

"This here's Frank Odum and R.W. Jessup. Ya'll know Madeline, don't you, fellas?"

I shook hands with Frank and R.W. Frank was thin and bony, while R.W. reminded me of a potato, his small features gathered in the center of his face. "Nice to meet you. Did any of you know Elijah Fenton?"

Frank laughed, and R.W. shook his head. "What you want to know about that ornery old cuss for?"

"I'm working on a case for his nephew, Nathan."

Horace nodded. "Nice boy. Not like the rest of 'em."

"Not like Elijah, that's for dang sure," Frank said. "Thought he was better than anybody else, all on account of him having some rich relative in France."

R.W. took a sip of his coffee. "Always thought that was a lie."

"Putting on airs, building that big old pile of rocks he called a castle, saying he was descended from French nobility. Who'd wanna be French, that's what I want to know."

"They make good mustard," Horace said, and the other two men looked at him askance.

"Mustard?" Frank said. "What's that got to do with anything?"

"French's mustard."

"Are you trying to make a joke?"

I got the conversation back on track.

"So Elijah was upset when his nephew Aaron married a local girl?"

Frank continued the story. "Lord, yes. See, Elijah never married."

"Too ornery," R.W. said.

"So he thought of Nathan and Aaron as his sons.

He'd picked out some rich gal from somewhere up in Virginia."

"I'm surprised he didn't order one from France," Horace said, which earned him another look from his cronies.

"Who's telling this?" Frank said.

"Go on, go on. Pardon me."

"But Aaron had already taken up with the Dewey girl. Never heard such a fuss. And nothing wrong with the Deweys. A nice family. That girl of theirs was right good-looking, too, so I don't know why Elijah was so dead set against her. He thought he was somewhat of a ladies man. Never could see it, myself, but he squired quite a few women around. None of 'em would have him, though, even with all his fortune."

"Wasn't he sweet on that Lever woman, the one what just died?" R.W. asked.

Horace laughed. "Now that would've been a pair! I think she told him what he could do with his money. Probably the only one to stand up to the old cuss, except for Aaron."

"Elijah wanted to date Amelia Lever?" I asked.

"Yup. He was pretty wild when he was in his twenties, and she wasn't bad-looking at nineteen. But like I said, she didn't want anything to do with him."

I took a few minutes to absorb that little nugget of information.

"Least the Dewey girl got the castle," R.W. said.

"Yeah. You hear that whirring noise?"

I listened, puzzled, until Frank's thin face wrinkled with laughter.

"That's old Elijah's spinning in his grave."

Nathan had told me Elijah left enough money for

Tori to live in the chateau. "Did something happen to change how Elijah felt about Tori?"

"Yeah, I think there at the end, he didn't like the way Aaron treated her."

When I returned to my booth, Jerry was grinning.

"What?" I said.

"You should have seen their faces when you walked away." Jerry widened his eyes and let his mouth hang open in what I'm sure he thought was a comical depiction of male lust.

"Ha, ha."

"Nudging each other, tongues flapping."

"Shut up."

He poured more ketchup on his fries. "You made their day. Find out anything?"

"Pretty much what I already knew. Elijah didn't have any children, so he took a lot of interest in his nephews' lives. He'd picked out a wife for Aaron and got a little miffed when Aaron married Tori. Oh, and the fellas say he tried to date Amelia Lever."

"You're kidding."

"Nope."

"A match made in heaven."

"Tried to date her. She turned him down."

"And he was such a catch."

"Horace and company think Aaron was an abusive husband, though."

"No wonder Tori jumped when she saw me. Oh, check this out. That might be Valerie Banner."

A small young woman with a large bag slung over one shoulder walked across the street. She came into Deely's, took a quick look around, and went right to our booth, her bright blue eyes sparkling.

"Mrs. Fairweather, hello! I'm Valerie Banner."

"Madeline, please." We shook hands, and I introduced Jerry, who stood to shake her hand. "Nice to meet you, Ms. Banner."

"Call me Valerie," she said. "I'll just slide in and sit next to you." She arranged herself and her large bag next to Jerry. She looked very young, her long black hair pulled back with a head band, and she was dressed all in black: black jeans, tee shirt, jean jacket, and boots. "Jerry, are you related to Des?"

"My older brother."

"Small world! He and my Uncle Jake are really good friends."

Jerry snapped his fingers. "Jake Banner. I knew I'd heard that name before."

"Only your brother doesn't have a lot of time to run around with Jake these days, does he? Isn't he on some world tour?"

"He's in China with the Parkland Symphony right now. I think it's a two week tour."

"I know he's loving every minute." She dug in her bag and brought out a digital camera. "But I don't want to waste your time, Madeline. Let me get a quick photo."

"Here?"

"Sure. The light's good. You look amazing, by the way."

"Thanks. You said you knew what I looked like. I'm curious about that."

She took a few pictures, examined the results, and nodded. "Jake told me."

Oh, great. No doubt her uncle knew me from pageants. But what she said next surprised me.

"Jake's into all sorts of paranormal things, so he knew all about Mantis Man."

Mantis Man, Celosia's Bigfoot.

She raised the camera. "Let me get just a few more. When you caught the woman who killed that movie director, Jake was all over that story because he thought you'd discovered the real Mantis Man."

Several people had dressed up as the Mantis, including one of Jerry's friends. "It was a hoax, Valerie."

She grinned. "Don't tell Jake that. He still believes it's out there. Anyway, he was really interested in what went on here, and that's how I know you."

I looked at Jerry, who just smiled. Valerie had yet to mention anything about my pageant past. She wasn't going for the beauty queen angle. She knew me from a case, a murder I had solved.

"Okay, I got some good shots." She put the camera back in her bag and took out a small tape recorder. "So tell me everything about your art."

Looking at Valerie Banner, I wouldn't have believed she was a competent reporter, but she was genuinely interested in what I had to say and asked insightful questions about me and my hopes for a career in art.

Then she asked, "So how difficult is it for a woman starting a detective agency in a small town?"

"I wanted to get away from the larger agencies in Parkland and really work on a more personal basis with people. I wanted to find things that they had lost, put lives back together. The fact that a murder occurred during my first visit was just fate. And I had the opportunity and the good fortune to solve that murder."

"But your first love is art?"

"Yes, I've always wanted to be an artist."

"And should your art career take off, do you plan to continue your investigations?"

"Yes," I said. "I can always make time for the things that are important to me."

She grinned. "I hear what you're saying. And believe me I know what it's like to have to prove yourself over and over. People look at me and think I'm working for my high school newspaper." She turned off the recorder and stuffed it and the camera back into her bag. "Okay, that should do it. Thanks so much."

"Thank you."

"And Jerry, thanks for the update on Des. I'll tell Jake. He'll want to go to China and start looking for dragons."

"Well, that wasn't so bad, was it?" Jerry asked me after Valerie had gone. "I did not hear the 'P' word one time."

"I know," I said. "You'd think by now I'd stop judging people on too little information."

"What do you mean?"

"I was ready to dismiss Valerie because she looked like a punk rock teenager. She's really quite a good reporter. You heard her say she knows what it's like to have to prove yourself over and over. I've had to do that practically all my life, and here I was, not willing to give her a chance."

"But you did, and I'll bet she's going to write a dynamite story."

I reached across the table to take his hand. "Thanks. I never would've entered that art show. I never would've had the opportunity for all this good publicity. This is one time I'm glad you're so sneaky."

"Wait till you see what I come up with next."

I must have really looked alarmed because he laughed and said, "Just kidding."

I TOOK JERRY TO the bookstore and headed back to Celosia Elementary. Rachel's art classes were a little more subdued and limited their questions to topics about art. Rachel explained she told them they would be graded on their behavior. I showed them how to shade drawings of fruit for a more three-dimensional look and illustrated ways to add perspective. Then they set about drawing a still life of fruit and toys Rachel had placed on a table in front of the room. As I walked around offering praise and suggestions, I couldn't help but think how much easier my life would've been if my mother had encouraged my artistic efforts instead of insisting I parade around on stage in a frilly and obscenely expensive dress, smiling stiffly and turning just so. My life might have been different, but if I'd had a successful art career, would circumstances have led me to Celosia and my own detective agency?

When the class was over, the students gathered their books and papers and lined up at the door. Several of them wanted me to sign their notebooks, so I borrowed a marker from Rachel and signed as many as I could before Norma Olsen arrived to take the classes back to their rooms. She was still beaming.

"How's everything working out for you?" I asked.

"Couldn't be better. This is a wonderful class, and we've had some good discussions about Mrs. Lever and what happened to her."

I couldn't help but notice Ronald Brown roll his eyes. "I'm glad to hear that."

"And we so appreciate you coming to talk with the

class. I'm sure they had a wonderful time. Come along, boys and girls."

Rachel picked up the stray papers. "Thanks so much, Madeline. That was great."

"You're welcome. How's everything here today?"

"Business as usual." She rearranged the still life. "I have something to ask you, if I'm not being too forward."

She wants me to come back, I thought. Well, I enjoyed this. It might be nice to teach another class.

"I've entered Bron and Mag in the Little Miss Rainbow Pageant in Parkland and I was wondering if you'd consider coaching them."

Good grief. "No, I'm sorry."

"Not even for a few minutes, just to show them how to walk? They deserve a little special treatment. They've been through a lot in their short lives, and I'm constantly amazed by how well they adapt to difficult situations."

I thought perhaps her daughters had health issues. "Difficult situations?"

She pushed her hair back, dislodging the little ear cuff long enough for me to see a slight "V" shaped notch in her ear. It wasn't something I would've been sensitive about, but then, I wasn't as high-strung as Rachel Sigmon. Maybe I wasn't being fair. I often found my looks to be a hindrance in my job.

She rearranged the cuff. "Their father left me, and the divorce proceedings have been rough on all of us. He still sees them, but I'm the one who deals with everything. But being a single mom has its advantages, and the girls have been wonderful. You could at least meet them. Then I know you'd want to work with them."

"Rachel, I know you haven't had an easy time, but every mother who puts her daughter in a pageant thinks her child is amazing."

Rachel's eyes narrowed. "If you had a child, you'd understand."

"You're exactly right."

"I want you to meet them."

I couldn't see any graceful way out of this. "I'm going to talk to Mrs. Dorman after school, and then maybe I'll have time to meet them."

"Come by my house. Do you have my number? Just call and come by any time. Come this afternoon."

"All right," I said. "But I'm not promising anything."

"Just meeting you will be a thrill, and maybe it will inspire them."

Just what I wanted to be, a shining example of queen-ness.

AFTER THE STUDENTS had been dismissed, I went to Mrs. Lever's room. Mrs. Dorman was sitting in the empty classroom eating a cup of yogurt.

"Mrs. Dorman?"

She blinked like a turtle suddenly coming into a patch of sunlight. "Yes?"

"May I ask you a few questions about Mrs. Lever?"

"I suppose so."

"Could you tell me what happened yesterday?"

She sighed. "Amelia was her usual self. I do remember her asking me if I'd seen her cigarettes. Asking is too polite a word. She demanded to know where they were." Mrs. Dorman stirred her yogurt. "I told her since I never touch the filthy things, I had no idea. She found them in her pocketbook, of course. She kept everything in these great big saddlebags—which reminds me. One of them is still in our storage closet. What should I do with it? I thought her sons would come get all her things."

"I'll be glad to take it to them," I said.

"Thank you. I want it out of my sight. It reeks of tobacco." She ate a spoonful of yogurt and then regarded me with her pale eyes. "It doesn't do any good to speak ill of the dead, but Amelia Lever was not a kind woman, and I can't pretend I liked her." She gestured with her spoon. "It's in that closet there."

I went to the closet and pulled out a large, heavy canvas bag. It bulged with papers. "Is this some of the kids' work?"

"Just leave those on a desk. I'll take care of them."

I put the papers on the nearest desk. "Working with Norma Olsen must be a nice change for you, then."

"She's all right. She talks to the students as if they were in kindergarten, though. And she's always laughing and playing games. Too silly for me."

I imagined everything and everyone was too silly for Mrs. Dorman. I thanked her and took my treasure out to the car. I'd take it to the Lever boys, but first, I was going to have a look. Sure enough, the bag smelled like the inside of an old muffler. I found two packs of cigarettes and a lighter, several packages of Bufo cards she'd probably taken from students, a bottle of pills marked K-Dur, a tube of the dark violet lipstick, a date book, and a photograph of a small boy with a distinctive Buster Brown haircut. Had to be one of the boys. The name "Rusty" was printed on the back along with the year the photo was taken, almost thirty years ago. I looked through the date book. The last day of every month had a big red "R" written on it. "R" for Rusty? Maybe the Lever boys would know.

But the most interesting thing I found was a piece of paper folded up in the back of the date book. It was a copy of Elijah Fenton's riddle.

MARSHALL AND Kevin Lever were listed in the phone book. Their address was Country Dale Apartments, B and C. I didn't find them there, so I drove to Amelia's house, a large brick Colonial style home near the school. When I got out of the car, I heard lively country music playing. The Lever boys were mourning in their own peculiar fashion. I went up to the front door and rang the bell. The music stopped. I heard muffled voices. The door opened, and Marshall Lever looked out, a transformed Marshall Lever. Gone was the unflattering hairstyle. Marshall now sported a short razor-cut style that changed his face from sad hangdog to male model. Gone was the flannel shirt. He wore a crisp white shirt, gray slacks, and a gray silk tie.

"Yes?"

"Madeline Maclin. We spoke at the PTA meeting. I was asked to return some of your mother's things."

"Oh," he said. He turned and called over his shoulder. "It's someone from the school, Kevin."

"Did she come for the textbooks?" Kevin called back.

"Yes," I said.

Marshall Lever opened the door wider. "Please come in. Excuse the mess. We're remodeling."

The house was dark and smelled of fresh paint. The

rug was an ugly forest green. The furniture was standard, unappealing. Ugly landscapes decorated the paneled walls. Several cardboard boxes filled with clothes were piled on the sofa.

Marshall indicated a stack of books on the coffee table. "We were just going through Mother's things, and we found these books that belong to the school. The new teacher might need them."

"I'll be glad to take them to her."

Kevin Lever came into the living room. His hair was also cut short. He had on paint-splattered overalls and sneakers.

"Marshall, come see if this is going to need another coat."

I followed the brothers down a short hall to another room. Here, Kevin had painted the paneling light blue, and the dark carpet had been torn up to reveal a hardwood floor.

"Quite an improvement," I said.

"We'd been trying to convince Mother we could make it look better," Kevin said. "She never wanted us to change anything."

"We're going to redo the whole house before the wedding," Marshall said. "Kevin's decided he'd like to live here. I'm buying a house closer to Parkland."

"Who gets the congratulations?"

"We both do. We're marrying Wanda and Shawna Bleeker next month. I'm sorry to say if Mother were alive, she'd never allow it."

The twins had to be in their forties, so this was puzzling. "Allow it?"

Marshall sighed. "I know it seems crazy, but it was

JANE TESH   119

so much easier to go along with her than oppose her. She could be very aggressive."

"She didn't want you to marry?"

"Mother never liked the Bleeker family. She said they were gold diggers. Dad left us plenty of money, but not what you'd consider a fortune. I never understood why Mother thought the twins wanted to marry us for our money."

"And she controlled the money," Kevin said. "Dad always did what she said. We wouldn't get any of our inheritance unless we married the woman Mother chose."

"Of course we have money of our own," Marshall said, "and we'd decided to give up our inheritance. We were even planning to elope, but now we can have the big church wedding the girls wanted."

"Eloping seemed our only choice," Kevin said, "and then— well, if Mother had to go, this was a good time."

Marshall looked uncomfortable. "We're not dancing around with glee, but we have to admit it's a relief."

"I wish you all the best," I said. I took out the photograph. "Oh, one other thing. This must be a picture of you."

Marshall shook his head. "That's not me."

Kevin looked. "It's not me, either."

"It says 'Rusty' on the back. Do you know who that is?" They glanced at each other, their identical expressions devoid of emotion.

"Oh, yes. Rusty. One of Mother's students."

"He'd be about your age. Did you know him?"

"No. She'd have a favorite every now and then," Kevin said. "Excuse me. I've got a lot of work to do. Another coat, Marshall?"

Marshall nodded. "That should do it."

That should do it, all right, I thought as Kevin went down the hall.

"Was there anything else, Ms. Maclin?"

"No, thank you."

"Let me help you with those books."

Since neither Lever brother seemed inclined to take the picture, I put it in my pocket. Amelia won't need her date book, or that bottle of pills, either, I thought, so while Marshall carried the stack of textbooks out to my car, I quickly rummaged in Amelia's bag and took out the items I hoped would help solve this mystery—if there was a mystery, including her copy of the riddle. I took the Bufo cards, too.

Marshall told me good-by and went back into the house. I took out my cell phone and called Nathan Fenton. He didn't answer. It was almost five o'clock. I really didn't want to go to Rachel's house to meet Bron and Mag, but I didn't have a good excuse not to go.

I got into the Mazda, and as I was hooking my seat belt, my cell phone buzzed. Yay, I thought, when I saw the caller was Jerry. Here's my excuse.

"Mac, Georgia's asked me to watch the store while she goes to Parkland. I'll be locking up around eight, so go home and paint."

An even better excuse. "Great idea. I'll pick you up at eight."

"Bring pizza," he said.

TO EASE MY CONSCIENCE, I gave Rachel a call. "I'm sorry I can't come by today. Can we reschedule?"

Rachel's voice sounded peeved. "Well, we were beginning to wonder."

"How about tomorrow?"

"Bron has dance lessons, and Mag is going with some of her little friends to the Princess Spa. I'll check their schedules and get back to you."

Well, they'd be so much happier going to the Princess Spa, I'm sure.

At home, I took a closer look at the items from Amelia's book bag. The riddle was the same as Nathan's. From the way the paper was tightly folded and stuck at the back of her date book, I imagined Amelia, like Aaron Satterfield, had probably decided not to play along. The packs of Bufo cards hadn't been opened. I looked through the date book, but other than the big "Rs," the entries were the usual doctor and dentist appointments and a few reminders about school meetings.

I went upstairs and decided to work on one of the landscapes. My work was going so well, I lost all track of time until my phone rang. This time Jerry's voice sounded serious.

"Mac, there's been a little trouble at the store. You'd better come right over."

MY HEART DID a huge flop when I saw the ambulance and police cars parked in front of the bookstore. I'm not sure how many people I knocked over to get inside. All around the checkout counter looked as if it had been stirred by a very large stick. Jerry, rumpled and dusty, was talking with Nell's father, Chief Brenner of the Celosia Police Department.

My heart resumed its natural rhythm. "You okay?"

"Yeah," he said. "Some nut decided to make a mess. Hit me from behind."

Chief Brenner opened his small notebook. "Did you see anything?"

"I just caught a glimpse of him as he ran out," Jerry said. "Blue jacket, baseball cap pulled down low. Looked like a teenager."

Brenner wrote this down and flipped the notebook closed. "Any idea what he was after? Can you tell what's missing?"

The floor in front of and behind the counter was a tossed salad of books, magazines, newspapers, candy, baseball cards, and gaming dice. Jerry's eyes widened as he got a good look at the damage. "This is going to take a while."

"See if you can sort things out. I'll have a look outside."

"Mind if I come along?" I asked. "I have a personal interest in this."

He nodded. "Come on."

I went with him. "No money was taken?"

"The register was solid as a rock and full of cash. This kid must've been on something." We met another officer coming up the sidewalk. "Whatcha got?"

The officer held up an empty spinner rack. "Found this in the alley next to the hardware store. Doesn't belong to them. And they say they saw a teenage boy run past not long ago. Blue jacket, baseball cap."

"Sounds like our thief."

I recognized the rack. "We can check with Jerry, but I'm pretty sure that's the rack for Bufo cards."

Chief Brenner frowned. "Those frog cards? Well, now, that's interesting. Let's have a look in the alley."

It's misleading to call the area between the hardware store and the drug store an alley because the narrow lane is paved and decorated with flowerbeds. Many people use the alley, so a search for footprints and other clues turned up nothing.

We went back into Georgia's, and Jerry agreed the rack belonged to the store.

Chief Brenner took out his notepad again. "How many packs do you think you had, Jerry?"

"Each section can hold ten packs. Over a hundred, I'd say."

"You sell that many packs of cards?"

"Yes, it's a big thing with the kids right now, and a lot of adults have been buying them, too." He rubbed the back of his head.

"Are you sure you're all right?" I said.

"The paramedics checked. My head is secure."

Since Jerry nearly always hits his head, I don't worry as much as I used to. Still, I really didn't like the idea of someone attacking him in the store. "You'd think a bookstore would be safe."

"You see why I'm not bored?"

"Is there any place he might try to sell the cards?" Brenner asked.

"More than likely, he'll look through the packs and throw away the cards he can't use."

The chief put his pad away. "All right. We'll check around and see if he ditched them anywhere. Anything else we need to know about these cards?"

"The new cards have gold foil wrappers," Jerry said. "The older sets have green."

After about an hour, Chief Brenner's team finished their work, and Brenner said we could start putting the store back together. Jerry and I shelved the books and gathered up the magazines scattered on the floor. He called Georgia to tell her the news. He assured her we'd have things in order by the time she got back to Celosia.

Fortunately, the mess wasn't as bad as it looked. By nine o'clock, everything was back in place. Jerry ordered a pizza, and then locked the store. We sat down on the stools behind the counter.

"So how was your day?" Jerry asked.

"Not as exciting as yours. I talked with Mrs. Dorman and got a few clues from Amelia's book bag. I talked with the Lever brothers. They've had a makeover and can't wait to marry the women Amelia didn't like."

"Not much of a mystery, then."

"I'm not sure. Amelia had a copy of the riddle in her bag, so Elijah thought enough of her to include her in his treasure hunt. And she had several packs of Bufo cards. First I thought she'd taken them from her students, tossed them in her bag, and forgot about them, but now, I wonder if there's a connection to this theft."

"Maybe she had some sort of special card. Where are they?"

"At home. We can check them out when—" I stopped. "Packs of Bufo cards. 'Trust animals that live in packs.' Is that what Elijah meant? When did they first come out?"

"The first cards came out back in the spring, but they didn't really catch on until later."

"So Elijah would have known about them. And if there's a clue to the treasure in the cards—"

"Then that's why someone decided to steal all of them."

A knock on the door made us both jump.

"Pizza's here," Jerry said. He unlocked the door,

paid for the pizza, then let the boy out and locked the door. "We can picnic in the children's section."

I still had the picture of Rusty in my pocket. "My only other clue is this. It's not Kevin or Marshall. Someone at the school might know."

We sat on the carpet in the children's book section. Jerry wedged a slice of pizza out of the box. "Let me see the picture."

I slid Rusty's photo over. "According to what I've learned about Amelia, it's odd for her to keep anything the students give her."

"Well, this picture looks like it was taken several years ago. Check out that hairstyle and the plaid shirt."

"That's why I thought it might be Kevin or Marshall. They have to be in their forties."

"It's Amelia and Elijah's secret love child."

"Although that stretches my imagination, I won't know for sure until I find Rusty."

"Any other clues?"

"I haven't heard from Warwick yet. Maybe he'll find out something."

"Maybe he can create a gold watch in that mad scientist lab of his."

"Jerry."

"Don't growl. I've had a rough day."

I slid over and put my arms around him. "I can make your day much more pleasant."

He pushed the pizza box aside and rolled me over on the carpet. I had pulled off his tie and was unbuttoning his shirt when we heard the click of the lock and Georgia's voice.

"Looks like someone's celebrating."

We scrambled to our feet. "Just making sure Jerry's okay," I said.

She peered at us over her half glasses. "Well, carry on, you two. The store looks fine."

FOUR

OF COURSE, we didn't carry on. Jerry explained what had happened. Georgia was happy cash hadn't been stolen or the store seriously damaged. We took our pizza and went home. Then we carried on. Later that night, I had really strange dreams about Amelia Lever, Mrs. Dorman, and Rachel competing in a Miss Bufo Pageant. I must have tossed and turned because Jerry grumbled he'd already been attacked once, would I please pull in my elbows? When I finally woke up and found my way downstairs, Jerry was making pancakes for breakfast.

"The winner and still champion," he said.

"Sorry. Are you black and blue?"

"No more than usual." The phone rang, and he answered. "Oh, yeah, hi, Bilby. You did? That's great! Oh, wait, it's silver? No, it has to be gold. Yeah, sorry. The next time Mac and I come to Parkland, I thought I'd check at Del's. Okay, thanks." He hung up and turned back to the stove. "That was Bilby Foster. He found a watch with an 'S' on it, but the watch is silver instead of gold."

I sat down at the table and tried to untangle my hair. "Gee, too bad."

"I know you don't approve, but you heard Sylvie. It's got to be a watch."

"A fake watch."

"No, a real one."

"I hate to enable your scams, but why don't you get a plain gold watch and get someone to engrave an 'S' on it?"

He paused in the act of flipping a pancake and pointed the spatula at me. "I knew there was a reason I married you. That's a great idea."

"But after this, please, no more séances. Tell Flossie Mae and Sylvie that was the last report from Beyond."

"Not even one at Halloween?"

"No more. Ever. Pass the syrup."

He handed me the bottle. "I'll think about it. Your plans today?"

"I didn't hear from Nathan. I thought I'd stop by his apartment and see if everything's okay. We need to try the rest of the portraits at the chateau, and then I'll be asking about Rusty at school."

"And trying to avoid Rachel."

"No, I might as well meet her girls and get it over with."

"You know she wants you to coach her little darlings."

"If they can fit me in between ballet and pedicures."

We heard the familiar sound of two bicycles landing on the front lawn, and two voices raised in argument.

Jerry said, "I'd better make another batch of pancakes."

Austin and Denisha hurried into the kitchen. "Oh, wow, pancakes!" Austin said. "Can I have some?"

"Pull up a chair."

Austin wasn't ready to sit. He bounced around Jerry. "We heard Georgia's got robbed last night. Were you there? Did you see the robber?"

Send For
2 FREE BOOKS
Today!

I accept your offer!

Please send me two free
Mystery Library™ novels and
two mystery gifts (gifts worth
about $10). I understand that
these books are completely
free—even the shipping and
handling will be paid—and I am
under no obligation to purchase
anything, ever, as explained on the
back of this card.

414/424 WDL FMM5

Please Print

FIRST NAME

LAST NAME

ADDRESS

APT.#   CITY

STATE/PROV.   ZIP/POSTAL CODE

Visit us online at
www.ReaderService.com

"I was there, but all the thief got was a bunch of Bufo cards."

"No way!"

"He made a big mess, that's for sure. Three pancakes be enough?"

"For starters."

"Get some plates and forks for you and Denisha."

Denisha sat down next to me. "How's your case coming along, Madeline?"

"Kind of slow right now."

"Did Georgia hire you to find the missing cards?"

"I think the police are handling that."

"Well, our collection is almost complete. I hope that thief got nothing but regular cards."

Austin displayed his arm, which was covered with Bufo stickers. "Look. I've got the entire Toad Army."

"Austin likes to pretend those are tattoos," Denisha said.

"It's the next best thing," he said. "They really stay on."

"It looks stupid."

"You just say that because girls don't have tattoos."

"They do so! Penny Robins' mother has them all over."

Jerry plopped pancakes on their plates. "These are the Pancakes of Peace. Eat them and argue no more." Denisha snickered. Jerry got more butter out of the fridge. "When do you want to go to Parkland, Mac?"

"After we visit Tori again and check those other portraits. Maybe around lunchtime."

"Okay. Kids, I know the thief got away with Georgia's supply of cards, so while I'm in the big city, I'll pick up some more."

"Great," Austin said. "I want to be the first one in my class with a complete set."

He gulped down his pancakes and unwedged a large stack of Bufo cards from his pocket. "Hey, Madeline, you know how to play Fifty-Two Pickup?"

"Yes, Jerry's done to me that many times."

"Aww."

"I'm guessing you learned that from him?"

"Yeah, it's cool."

Denisha licked syrup off her fingers. "It's the silliest thing."

"No, it's cool. Come on, Madeline, pretend you don't know how."

"Okay. Ask me again."

"Do you know how to play Fifty-Two Pickup?"

"No, I don't."

He bent the pack back until the cards shot from his hand and scattered across the room. "Pick 'em up!"

From the way he laughed, Fifty-Two Pickup must be the funniest thing Austin had ever seen. Denisha sighed. "You don't even have fifty-two cards in that stack."

"Okay, then, it's Thirty-Six Pickup."

"And you have to pick them up yourself."

"I was going to." He gathered the cards, still chuckling. "I can't wait to show Ronald. Can I have some more pancakes?"

"Sure," Jerry said.

Denisha turned to me. "When are you going to come talk to our class about art, Madeline?"

"I'll see if I can schedule the other fourth grades with Mrs. Sigmon."

"She's a good teacher. She doesn't want her kids at Celosia Elementary, though."

"Maybe she thinks Parkland Academy is better for them."

"No, she didn't want Bronwen to have Mrs. Lever."

"Oh?"

"See, a lot of kids were scared of Mrs. Lever. You'd see them in the halls crying 'cause their names were on her list."

"Was Bronwen scared of her?"

"Oh, yes. Mrs. Lever had a very loud voice, and she'd use that tone, what do you call it? Like you didn't understand and she felt sorry for you, only not really. Con something."

"Condescending?"

"Yes, that's it. Like, 'Just because your mother's a teacher, don't expect special treatment. I don't expect you to know anything.' Stuff like that."

"You heard her say this?"

"I heard Bronwen telling some other kids at lunch. She said there was no way she was going to be in that class. She said she'd tell her mother, and her mother would move her to another school."

Austin sat back at the table. "I didn't want her, either. Now we'll get Ms. Olsen or Mrs. Culpepper or Mrs. Freedmont, only I hope I get Ms. Olsen because I think she'd be fun."

"You don't have to worry about that till next year."

"Yeah, but at least I don't have to worry about getting Mrs. Lever."

"She liked kids who weren't afraid of her. I wasn't afraid of her."

"That's because you never had her yet. Didn't you hear she had an electric paddle?"

Denisha rolled her eyes. "She did not."

"So Bronwen and Magwen left Celosia Elementary this year?" I asked.

"Oh, yes. Their mother does whatever they tell her to do."

"Wish my mom did whatever I tell her to do," Austin said, his mouth full.

"You wouldn't like it for long," Denisha said. "There's limits, you know."

"I don't like those girls, but Sparky Lawrence said Bron was going to have this huge birthday party with one of those moon walk castle things and pony rides and maybe a magician. You ought to go and do tricks for them, Jerry. Then I could go with you."

"No, thanks," he said. "I'm all out of balloon animals."

I had left Amelia's bag and its contents on the kitchen counter. I got out the unopened packs of Bufo cards and brought them to the table. "Let's see if there's anything special in these packs."

Austin and Denisha were more than happy to help out, even though they complained the cards smelled like cigarettes.

"Pew! Where'd you get these?" Austin said.

"Mrs. Lever, believe it or not."

"Not. How come the seal on this one's been reglued?"

I hadn't noticed. "Has it?"

"How can you tell?" Denisha asked.

"The Terrible Tadpole's leg is crooked."

Jerry and I peered at the seal, which resembled an

oversized sticker. Sure enough, the Terrible Tadpole, fanged and glowering, had one leg that didn't exactly line up with his foot.

"Somebody opened these and sealed them back up," Austin said. "But the cards are all in their wrappers. Guess whoever did it changed his mind."

Or put some special cards in, I thought. "Have the other packs been resealed?"

We checked them all. "Yup," Austin said. "Look. Bufo's eye is supposed to be over here."

On one sticker seal, Bufo appeared to be looking over his shoulder and at his sword at the same time. On another, one star in the pattern in his Cape of Justice didn't quite match the other stars.

"You really have to look close," Denisha said.

"How easy is it to rewrap the cards?" I asked.

Austin was glad to show me. "Real easy. The foil just folds back over. Can we open them for real?"

"Yes."

Jerry moved the breakfast dishes over so we could open all the packs and spread the cards out on the table.

Denisha frowned. "What exactly are we looking for?"

"I don't know," I said. "See anything out of the ordinary?"

We stared at the cards. "Nope," Austin said. "They're kind of pitiful, if you ask me. Not even a power card. There's a king card, though. That's neat, but it's not rare."

Denisha glanced at the clock above the sink. "We'd better get to school, Austin."

The kids thanked Jerry for the pancakes, and rode their bikes back down the driveway.

"Need a ride to the store?" I asked Jerry.

"Not today. Thought I'd lie around the house in my underwear watching TV and eating Cheetos."

"Thanks for the warning."

He grinned. "No, I'm going to play through the cantata before I make any decision about it."

"Don't feel obligated to take on a job you won't like."

"Oh, I've been thinking of other things I can do. We could still make the house into a bed and breakfast."

That had been Jerry's first plan for the house until he realized how much work was involved. "I think I have more than enough to keep me busy, thanks."

"What I'm really going to do is study these cards," he said. "We're missing something. I'll figure it out."

"Good," I said. "See you at lunchtime."

NATHAN FENTON LIVED in a small apartment on Ashland Drive. I rang the doorbell. When he opened the door, he looked startled.

"Oh, Madeline. I wasn't expecting you. The place is a wreck."

"That's okay," I said. "I just want to let you know how things are progressing."

"Of course. Come in."

Nathan hadn't been exaggerating. His place was a wreck. Stacks of papers leaned dangerously in all directions. The coffee table was covered with more papers and folders. On the small counter that separated the living room from the kitchen, more papers fought for space with dirty dishes, ashtrays, and empty pizza boxes.

He cleared off a chair. "The place looks awful, I know. It's all the paperwork for the camp. I'm trying to get a grant proposal finished, too, and sponsors for some of the kids. Please, sit down."

When I sat down, I noticed something else on the counter. Several packs of Bufo cards.

"Would you mind if I had a look at those?" I asked.

"Sure, go ahead."

I picked up one of the packs. I could tell by the uneven pattern on the seal that this pack had also been opened and resealed. I slid my thumbnail under the seal and opened the pack. I was glad to see the wrappers were green foil and not the stolen gold. Nathan as Bufo Card Thief was too much for my imagination.

"You're not a collector, are you?" I asked him.

"Collector?"

"The Bufo cards."

"Oh, those came in the mail. Some sort of free samples, I guess. I thought I'd save them for the camp and give those to the kids who can't afford them."

"When did you get them?"

"You know, I really don't remember."

"Before or after your uncle died?"

He stared at me. "What?"

"'Trust animals that live in packs.' I think this is part of the riddle."

"Packs like packs of cards? Really?" He frowned. "Come to think of it, Fiona asked about the cards, too, but I don't see how they'd have anything to do with the riddle. Bufo's a made up animal, not a real one, and Elijah wouldn't have known anything about kids' playing cards."

I thought Elijah had probably known everything that was going on. And the riddle didn't specify real animals. "It's worth a look. Can I take these with me?"

"Of course."

"I'm going back to the chateau today to check out the portraits. You're certainly welcome to join me."

Somewhere in the depths of all the paper, his phone rang, saving him from a reply. "Excuse me." He dug around until he found his phone and answered. "Yes? Oh, yes, I've got that information. It's in my office. One moment, please."

As he went into the other room, I took advantage of his absence to look around. The stacks of paper all had to do with safety, sanitation, food, and activities for a children's camp. The pizza box was from Mario's. The dishes were going to need sandblasting. And among the cigarette butts in the ashtray were two with distinctive purple lipstick stains. I picked up one of the cigarette butts and slipped it into my pocket. When I heard Nathan finish his conversation, I was back in the chair by the time he returned to the living room.

"My apologies, Madeline. That was the English teacher at Celosia High. She's helping me with the grant. Was there anything else?"

"I spoke with your cousin Aaron. He received the riddle, too, but says he has no interest in it." I wondered if Aaron had also received anonymous packs of Bufo cards, as well.

"That doesn't surprise me too much," Nathan said. "He doesn't need the money."

"I'm sorry he and Tori are having trouble."

Nathan's expression became guarded. "It's not likely they'll get back together."

"I mentioned you're welcome to join me at the chateau."

"Maybe later," he said. "You can imagine I'm very busy getting all this paperwork organized."

"I understand," I said. "And I promise I'm working on your case, even though I've been hired to solve Amelia Lever's death."

He blinked. "I thought she had a heart attack."

"She did, but there are some questions about that. Did you know her?"

His hands shook slightly as he straightened one of the stacks of papers. "I met her once or twice. She was Aaron's fifth grade teacher."

"Did you see her after Aaron left town?"

"I might have a few times, just around, you know. This really has nothing to do with anything! Are you going to solve the riddle in time, that's all I'm concerned about."

I started to say yes when he took a quick breath and said, "I'm sorry. That didn't sound right. I appreciate all you're doing, it's just, well, I'm really nervous about meeting the deadline."

"I understand."

"And the news about Mrs. Lever—after that business this summer with Josh Gaskins being poisoned—I'm sorry, I'm just not used to things like this happening in Celosia."

We were a quiet, happy little town until you moved here, I expected him to say. "It's entirely possible Mrs. Lever did have a heart attack."

"Well, that's very sad news. I'm sure her students will miss her." He had regained his calm. "I'd love for you to come out to the camp some day soon and see what I plan to do."

"I'd like that."

"Again, I apologize."

"Don't worry about it, Nathan."

Out in my car, I examined the cigarette butt more carefully. It was stained with exactly the same shade of lipstick Amelia Lever had been wearing. I hadn't noticed Fiona Kittering wearing lipstick or any sort of make up. Unless Nathan was cheating on Fiona with someone who wore this violent dark purple lipstick, and taking into account his reaction when I mentioned her name, Amelia Lever had been in his house not long before she died.

Why?

I was still puzzling over this when I stopped by Celosia Elementary to show Thad Murphy the picture of the mysterious Rusty.

"Do you know who this is?"

Thad Murphy examined the photo and handed it back, shaking his head. "I don't recognize this boy."

"I thought it might be one of Amelia Lever's sons, but they say no."

"I've been principal here eight years. Check with some of the people who've worked here longer. Mrs. West might know."

Eloise West was the school secretary, a pleasant-looking older woman with short white hair. She peered at the photo through her green-framed half glasses. "That's Ronald McIntire. We called him 'Rusty.' A very sweet little fellow. My goodness, I hadn't thought of him in years. Such a pity."

"What happened?"

She kept her gaze on the picture. "He came from a dreadful home situation. The parents were always fighting. He was extremely bright, but they never gave permission for him to have any of the accelerated classes or go on field trips. They said they didn't want him 'getting ideas.' They were poor and ignorant and resented any sort of education. Rusty was absent more days than he was here." She sighed and handed the picture to me. "Then one day he didn't come back. The family moved away and we never saw him again. We had a request for his records from a school in Virginia, and that's the last we heard of him."

"Was Mrs. Lever his teacher?"

"I believe she had him when she taught fourth grade."

"Any idea why she kept his picture?"

"No. That doesn't sound like Amelia. She was not a sentimental person. In fact, she always gave away the gifts the children brought her."

"Did she have any contact with Rusty's parents? Any conferences?"

"They never came to school. We'd get angry phone calls or badly misspelled notes. I do remember her saying it was a crime that such a bright student was handicapped by ignorant parents and she wished she could've done more for him."

"Mrs. West, were you the secretary when Aaron Satterfield was in school?"

"Oh, I remember Aaron. He was quite a handful."

"Was he also one of Mrs. Lever's students?"

"I believe he was."

"Did she show any particular interest in him?"

"No, Rusty was the only one whose situation seemed to upset her."

I thanked Mrs. West and went back to Thad Murphy's office. He didn't look happy.

"About your investigation, Ms. Maclin. Can we safely assume Mrs. Lever's death was accidental?"

"I have a few more leads to follow," I said.

"I don't like having any sort of unfinished business associated with the school. When do you think you might have an answer?"

"I don't know. I'm working as quickly as possible."

I had unfinished business, too, with Rachel Sigmon. I found her on the playground, talking with another teacher. On the field, a group of students screamed through a game of kickball. When a foul ball landed on someone's head, the teacher hurried to referee.

"Hello, Madeline," Rachel said. "I heard about the robbery at Georgia's Books. Is Jerry okay?"

"Yes, thanks."

I wasn't surprised she'd heard about the incident. "A teenager stole some cards."

"Stole some cards? Baseball cards, you mean?"

"No, those Bufo the Warrior Toad cards all the kids are collecting."

"That's really odd. He didn't take anything else? He didn't demand money, or try to take the cash register?"

"Just the cards."

"Do the police know who it was?"

"They didn't get much of a description."

"Well, I'll tell you who I'd suspect. Bobby Berkely. He's one of our worst little hoodlums. The police have caught him breaking into cars and spray-painting buildings, you name it."

"A teenager?"

"Yes, he's probably sixteen, seventeen."

"Blue jacket? Baseball cap?"

"That sounds exactly like him."

"Thanks," I said. "I'll check into that. When can we reschedule my visit?"

"Oh," she said with a dismissive wave of her hand. "You know, Madeline, I've been a real jerk about all this. You don't have to do anything for the girls. I'd still like you to meet them some time, but I've had a little time to think, and I was being a real stage mother. I promise you I'm not like that."

"You just want the best for them. I understand. Did you tell me the girls go to Parkland Academy?"

"Yes, they love it there. They get so much more individual attention."

"Was Bronwen supposed to be in Mrs. Lever's class?"

"I felt Mrs. Lever was much too strict for a sensitive child like Bron. Besides, I'd already planned for the girls to change schools." She lowered her voice. "Their father knew he wasn't allowed on the grounds of Celosia Elementary, yet he kept coming around and being a pest. It was easier for me to move the girls."

"I see."

"I do want to schedule you for another art class, though. The students really enjoyed your visit. Maybe when you finish your investigation. How's it coming along?"

"A few more leads to follow."

The other teacher came back, her arm around a

tearful boy with a nosebleed. "Mrs. Sigmon, would you mind watching my class while I take Blake to the school nurse?"

"No problem. Excuse me, Madeline."

I sat down at one of the picnic tables at the edge of the playground. Ms. Olsen's class came galloping out for their recess. Ronald Brown saw me and came over.

"Hey."

"Hey yourself."

He sat down beside me. "I just wanted to let you know I think you're hot."

"Thank you."

"Have you solved the murder yet?"

"What makes you think there's been a murder, Ronald?"

"You wouldn't be hanging around here if old lady Lever just keeled over. Think somebody offed her?"

"I'm still investigating."

"So you're gonna find out what really happened?"

"Eventually."

"Got any clues?"

"Not very many."

He leaned forward and lowered his voice. "I've got one. Want to hear it?"

"Sure."

"Well, there was this one day when Mrs. Sigmon and Mrs. Lever had it out in the hall. I was hoping they'd start fighting. Mrs. Lever could whip Mrs. Sigmon's butt."

"What were they fighting about?"

"I don't know. It didn't make sense to me."

"Did anyone else hear them?"

"Nah, just me. I had to stay in during recess just for

flipping Timothy off. He flipped me off first, only he didn't get caught. Mrs. Lever said, 'You don't know anything about it,' and Mrs. Sigmon said, 'You're lying because you want the money,' and Mrs. Lever said, 'Oh, you won't get it, ha, ha.' Only she didn't say, 'Ha, ha,' she just laughed real mean."

Ronald must have heard Rachel and Amelia arguing about the grant proposal. "I think Mrs. Lever was real mean to a lot of people, Ronald."

"Yeah, that's what makes it so hard to figure out who did it, right?"

"Right."

"Well, she wasn't real mean to me. I liked her because she was tough, you know, like a Marine drill sergeant or something. Ms. Olsen is a flake. She plays this stupid drippy music in the classroom and wants us to blow bubbles and tell her our feelings."

"Sorry to hear that."

He sighed. "It's gonna be a long year."

Ms. Olsen must have realized one of her students was missing. She came up to the picnic table, her round face slightly puzzled.

"Ronald, you shouldn't be bothering Mrs. Fairweather."

I got up. "It's my fault, Ms. Olsen. I was asking Ronald some questions about his father. We met at PTA, and I thought I recognized his dad from my college days. Seems we both went to the same university."

Her expression cleared. "Oh, well, isn't that nice? Ronald, you need to run and get some fresh air, dear."

Ronald grinned at me. "That was smooth. Catch you later."

"Smooth?" Norma Olsen said as Ronald ran down to the ball field.

I shrugged. "Must be some kind of slang. How are you getting along?"

"Oh, this is the most wonderful class. I really hate to say this, but Amelia was much too strict with them. I feel they've blossomed now that she's gone."

"When did you last see Amelia?"

"Last spring, when I thought she was going to retire. I didn't actually see her. She called me to say she'd changed her mind. I was so looking forward to teaching here it just about broke my heart. She was so mean-spirited. I think she stayed on to spite me."

"Did she have a particular grudge against you?"

"I never did a thing to her except exist. Some people go through life offended by every little thing, you know."

"Was there anyone else who wanted her job?"

"I'm sure there were some other people, but I know I was first choice for the position. I'd discussed it with the superintendent and with Thad, and they both agreed I had all the proper credentials. All I had to do was wait until Amelia retired. But I couldn't wait forever. I had to take a job at Baby Brains Day Care, which is a nice place to work, don't get me wrong."

So did you do something to hasten the process? "Amelia had health problems. It seems to me she would've wanted to retire."

"No one knows why she was hanging on so long. I know I took it personally, which was wrong of me, but as I said, she practically laughed in my face."

"She didn't give you any reason?"

"No. All she said was she'd decided to stay on another year."

"Did she need the money?"

"I doubt it. Her husband ran one of the larger mills in town. I'm sure he left her plenty." Her plump cheeks turned pink. "Well, now, I do remember something else. She said she didn't want to turn her class over to someone who lived in a fantasy land. I thought that was extremely harsh. Just because I like to be surrounded by pretty things doesn't mean I live in a fantasy land. She liked to make it sound as if I'd lost touch with reality. I have different teaching methods, that's all. Do you have an objection to rainbows?"

"No, I like rainbows."

"And children do, too. Just because they've turned eleven or twelve doesn't mean they have to become completely adult in everything they do. I like to have fun, and I believe children learn better when they're having fun. Amelia was too strict, that's all there is to it."

"I understand she had good test results."

Norma's cheeks turned an even deeper shade of pink. "Oh, those awful tests! Everyone hates them. The poor kids get so stressed. We all do. I wish they'd do away with any sort of testing and just let the children learn. Children learn so much better in a natural and free environment where they can realize their own potential." She sighed. "But that's not going to happen. That's really the only thing I don't like about teaching."

And probably that was one of the things Amelia didn't like about Norma. She figured Ms. Olsen would be too soft on the students and their important end of year grades would slip. Or did that mean anything to

Amelia? As for a natural and free environment, I knew what most normal kids would do. Run wild and free. "I hope the class does well for you, Norma."

"Thanks," she said. "I'm going to do my best. We'll make good things happen." She gazed past me to the playground. "Now who left that book out by the swings? I hope it's not one of our new library books."

When she said that, I realized I still had the stack of textbooks Marshall Lever had put in the back seat. While Norma Olsen sent one of her students to retrieve the library book, I thanked her for her time, said good-by and went back to my car. The stack of books had fallen and scattered over the back seat. I saw a piece of paper between two of them. I tugged the paper free. It was a grant proposal, just like some of the papers I'd seen at Nathan's house. Had Amelia Lever been trying to sabotage Nathan's plans, or was this paper left over from one of her other schemes? Two pages were stapled together, and on the second page I found, "Nathan, you need to check this" written at the top in firm dark letters. I took Amelia's date book out of my pocketbook and compared the handwriting. It was the same. Now I had to revise my theories. Was Amelia trying to help Nathan achieve his goal?

I kept the paper. I took the books to the office and went to my car. I keep a Celosia phone book under the passenger seat, so I looked up Berkely. There were two Berkelys listed. The first number I called belonged to a woman who informed me I wanted the Other Berkelys. I could hear the capital letters and the disdain.

"Whatever it is you want, they're the ones to call," she said. "I'm not certain which one's more useless, the mother or the son."

A woman also answered the second number, but her voice was weary and not quite coherent. "What?"

"I'd like to speak to Bobby Berkely, please."

"What's the little jerk done now?"

Not a very good beginning. "Are you his mother?"

"Wish to God I wasn't."

"Would you happen to know where he is?"

"Of course I know where he is. He's at PR where he belongs. Who is this?"

"I'm Madeline Maclin. I'm investigating a robbery at the bookstore. What's PR?" Somehow I doubted she meant Public Relations.

"Parkland Reform School. Going to be there until Christmas." She belched and hung up.

With such a charming home life, Bobby was probably happy to be sent away. I called Chief Brenner, and he confirmed the information.

"If he was in town, he'd be our prime suspect," he said, "but his mother's right. He's serving time."

"No other leads?" I asked.

"No."

I drove home. On the way, I wondered if I had any sort of case. But I had answers to two questions. Rusty was another Ronald, Ronald McIntire, and Ronald Brown was the only person in town who had liked Amelia Lever.

Although I couldn't rule out Nathan. Not yet.

As I WALKED UP the porch steps, I heard Jerry at the piano playing "Noel," and I paused at the door of our parlor, which doubled as a séance room and a music room, to listen. I could tell Jerry was adding his own spin to the familiar carol. At one point, he added a little blues riff and finished with a calypso beat.

I applauded. "The church will love it."

He turned on the bench and grinned. "I call it 'Multicultural Noel, A Carol For the New Age.'"

"Any luck with the cards?"

"Not yet."

I took Nathan's packs out of my pocketbook. "Well, guess what? Nathan received some packs in the mail. Same resealed seals."

"Okay, now I know we're on to something."

I took out my phone. "I'm giving Aaron a call. Maybe he got some packs, too."

While Jerry spread the cards out on his séance table, I found Aaron's number in my pocketbook. Once again, I got his secretary, who said she'd have Aaron call me at his earliest convenience. I thanked her and closed my phone. "Find anything?" I asked Jerry.

He shook his head. "I can't see anything unusual about these."

"How about compared with Amelia's?"

"Just your standard packs with a few good cards thrown in. Nothing special."

I pointed to one card. "What about this king card? Austin mentioned that."

"Well, it's a good card, but it's no Tongue of Death."

I took a closer look at the king card. The Bufo card showed Bufo as King of the Toads, complete with robe, crown, and scepter. He had a very smug look on his wide face. "King of All Four Corners of the World" was written in fancy gold script above his head.

"Seems like there are duplicates of a lot of these cards, but only one king card."

"I'll keep looking," Jerry said.

I had another thought. "I wonder if Elijah's lawyer knew about this." I still had Misty May's number, too, and gave her a call. Like Aaron, she was not available, so I left a message with her secretary to please get in touch with me today, if possible. "Ready for the chateau?" I asked Jerry.

He gathered the cards into a stack. "You bet. I looked through some of my stuff and found some programs and ticket stubs for Tori. Maybe we can convince her to go to the opera with us next time."

"That's a great idea."

As we drove to Satterfield Drive, Jerry asked about Amelia Lever. "I've got too many questions and not enough answers," I said.

"Suspects?"

"A whole pile of them. Marshall and Kevin have a great motive. They've been under their mother's control all their lives, and now that she's dead, they're free to do whatever they want and marry the women they want. Norma Olsen seems really sweet, but she was very upset when Amelia didn't retire. If she killed Amelia, now she has the job she wanted. Even Rachel's a suspect. She says she moved her girls to Parkland Academy because of their father, but you heard what Denisha said this morning about Bron being afraid of Mrs. Lever. And one of Amelia's students heard Rachel arguing with Amelia over the art grant. That gives Rachel two reasons to be mad at Amelia. Then there's Mrs. Dorman and the rest of the faculty."

"Okay, they've all got motives. What about opportunity?"

I stopped at a red light at the intersection of Maple

and Main. "Rachel and Jacey were the only ones on the loading dock when Amelia died. I need to hear what Warwick has to say—if he found out anything. It's possible she really died of a heart attack. And then there's the problem of Nathan."

"Nathan? How's he involved?"

"I'm pretty sure Amelia was at his apartment not long before she died."

"Nathan and Amelia. Give me a moment to visualize."

"Unless Nathan's decided to wear Purple Passion lipstick when no one's watching. I found her brand of cigarette butts with her distinctive purple lipstick on them, and I found a paper like the ones at Nathan's house in a stack of Amelia's textbooks."

"Why would she be visiting Nathan?"

"A better question would be why did she write, 'Nathan, you need to check this' on the paper."

"A threat?"

"No, I think she was trying to help him."

"We're talking about Amelia Lever here, hated and feared throughout the land."

"Yes, but Ronald Brown liked her, and I'm pretty sure the mysterious Rusty liked her. There could be a good reason she wanted to help Nathan."

"Or ruin his chances. She seemed to be good at sabotage."

"If that's the case, then Nathan has a motive, too."

Tori must have been waiting at the door because she opened it the minute we rang the bell.

"Come in, come in! Oh, Jerry, I love your tie!"

Jerry had worn a blue tie with yellow light bulbs on it. "I hope it'll give us some bright ideas."

"I love it! Can you stay for lunch? I've fixed something."

"Sure, that sounds nice. And I brought some things for a new scrapbook."

She was enchanted with the programs and ticket stubs. "Oh, this is wonderful! I never thought about making an opera scrapbook." She examined each program. "*Paul Bunyan, Faust, Tales of Hoffmann.* You'll have to tell me what all these are about."

"I'll be glad to."

"These must have been fantastic productions."

"Even better live and in color. You'll have to come with us and see one."

"Oh," she said. "Well, maybe."

"You'd really like *Tales of Hoffmann.* It's like a bizarre fairy tale."

She nodded. I could tell she was afraid he was going to pull her out the door and make her go see the opera right this minute. She set the programs and ticket stubs on a small table in the foyer. "But first let's continue our treasure hunt!" She practically bounced down the hallway. "Now, where did we stop? Oh, yes, Aunt Rescinda."

Jerry took down the portrait of the scowling Aunt Rescinda. There was nothing behind the picture, nothing hidden in the frame, and nothing very inspiring about the aunt's angry look.

"She must not have wanted her picture painted," Jerry said as he maneuvered the portrait back on its hook. "Who's next?"

"Elijah's cousin, Barnaby Fenton. Oh! Oh! There's a bird in the tree!"

I thought Tori was having an episode until I realized she was pointing to a small brown bird painted on the tree behind Cousin Barnaby.

"Is that the sparrow from ancient times?"

Jerry took a closer look. "It could be. How ancient is Cousin Barnaby?"

"I think he lived in the eighteen hundreds."

"Do you see a river?"

"What's that just behind his head?"

Jerry took the picture down so we could see. Cousin Barnaby, like all of the other relatives, was scowling. He stood with his hands folded. He had on a fine black suit and tie, and his white hair fanned out like a lion's mane. He'd been painted outside, or in front of a nature backdrop. In the background, a dark flow of water cascaded over rocks and around trees.

"West to east?" Jerry asked.

I looked around. "Tori, which direction does your house face?"

"North," she said.

"So if we're standing here, and your front door is behind us, then the river in this picture is going west to east."

"Oh, my goodness, this is it! This is it!"

I thought she was going to explode. "Take it easy. It has to fit the rest of the riddle."

"'Listen where the portrait lies,'" Jerry quoted. "Okay, I'll listen." He put his ear to the wall where the portrait had been hanging. "I hear nothing but stone."

She giggled and actually touched his arm. "Why

don't you bring the portrait to the dining room? We can examine it while we have lunch."

Tori had made salad, some sandwiches, and had a variety of cookies. We put Cousin Barnaby in a chair and looked at him while we ate.

Tori nibbled on a lettuce leaf. "I can't believe we're so close."

I wanted to make sure she understood about the so-called treasure. "You know anything we find goes to Nathan."

"Yes, and I want him to have it. This has been so exciting for me, though. I haven't had this much fun in years."

"Mac and I have this kind of fun all the time," Jerry said. "You're welcome to join us."

She gave him a wistful smile. "That's so sweet of you, but I'm fine right here."

I decided to come right out and ask the question. "Tori, are you afraid to leave your house?"

The lettuce leaf trembled in her hand. "No."

"Maybe you need something to wear? We could go shopping."

"No, thank you. I can't, that's all."

She looked as if she might cry. Jerry changed the subject. "Tori, are you sure that's Cousin Barnaby?"

"Why do you ask that?"

"I've been thinking. The riddle says, 'And listen where the portrait lies.' What if it means 'lies' like 'not tell the truth'?"

"But what about the sparrow and the river? They're both in this picture."

"Is that really Cousin Barnaby?"

She gave the picture another long look. "Well, I don't know. I'm just going by what Aaron said."

"Maybe something else in the picture is a lie," I said.

She brightened. "Like those pictures that have all sorts of things wrong in them, or hidden pictures." She hopped up and put her little nose almost on the portrait. "What could it be?"

"Tori," I said, "why won't Nathan come to the chateau?"

She sat back. "He never liked coming here. He said it was too big and gloomy."

"But having to solve this riddle by Monday, I would've thought he would have been over here every day examining the portraits. And he knows his family better than I do. Why hire a stranger?"

She wouldn't look at me. "He's not welcome here."

"Why not?"

"He's just not."

I didn't quite understand. Nathan, like Jerry, was not a threatening-looking man. "Are you afraid of him?"

"No. I—I'm mad at him."

"What did he do?"

Her voice caught. "I don't want to talk about it."

"Okay."

"Are there any more chocolate cookies?" Jerry asked.

She gave him a shaky smile. "I think so."

My cell phone buzzed. "Excuse me," I said. I left the table and went out into the hallway, mainly to give Tori time to recover. "Hello?"

It was Aaron Satterfield. "Sorry I didn't get back to you sooner, Ms. Maclin. Someone tried to break into my home last night. I've been down at the police station making sure they have all the details."

"Are you all right?"

"Yes, fine. I wasn't home at the time, and I have a good security system."

"Any idea why your home was targeted?" I asked, thinking it would be an amazing coincidence if he said, "Yes, to steal my Bufo cards." But he didn't.

"Unfortunately, a lot of homes in the neighborhood have been broken into lately. The police say the thief or thieves are after TVs and DVD players, the usual. What can I do for you?"

"Mr. Satterfield, did you receive some packs of Bufo cards in the mail recently?"

"Bufo cards?"

"Kids' trading cards with pictures of dressed up frogs on them."

He gave one of his amused snorts. "Oh, those things. My secretary said something about that. She checks all my mail."

"Do you still have them?"

"No, I told her to throw them away. They must have been sent here by mistake. Why? What's your interest in them?"

"They might have been part of Elijah's game."

Another snort. "Then I definitely didn't want them. Sounds like his way of saying, 'Jump when I tell you to.' Was there anything else?"

"Do the police have a description of the thief?"

"No. Why? Is this relevant to Elijah's riddle?"

"I don't know."

"Just a random break in, Ms. Maclin. I can't imagine how it would connect."

I couldn't, either. He said good-by and hung up. My

phone buzzed a second time. Misty May was returning my call. "Another question, Ms. Maclin?"

"Yes," I said. "Did part of Elijah's game involve packs of Bufo cards?"

"Bufo cards? The ones with the frogs on them?"

"That's right."

"Well, that's odd," she said. "The last time I spoke with him, he gave me a card like that. I remember because he laughed, and he didn't laugh often."

"Do you still have it?"

"Yes."

"It might be helpful if I could see it," I said.

"I could mail it to you."

This was Thursday afternoon. I probably wouldn't get the card until Saturday, which was cutting it a bit fine. "Rossboro's a short drive from Celosia, isn't it? Why don't I stop by later today? Would that be all right?"

"Of course. My office is on the corner of Clover and Fourth. I'll be here till six."

I closed my phone and went back into the dining room. As I expected, Jerry had cheered Tori with some sleight of hand tricks. He pulled a cookie from behind her ear.

"See? Told you there was another one."

"That's amazing! You should be on TV."

Despite the brightness in her eyes, she looked tired and frail. I thought we should give her a little space. "I may have a lead in this case. You won't mind if we come back later, Tori?"

"Oh, my, no. While you're gone, I'll continue to look for clues to the riddle."

"Good idea."

We left her staring earnestly at Cousin Barnaby.

"Did you make that up about having a lead?" Jerry asked as we walked down the dark hall to the front door.

"No, Misty May has a Bufo card in Rossboro we need to see. And I felt Tori had had enough for today."

"Rossboro. That's convenient. Didn't you want to check it out?"

"We can go right now."

Jerry opened the door for me. "Mac, I need to go to Parkland, remember? Check with Del?"

"Why don't we see if there are some pawn shops in Rossboro?"

"Del will probably have exactly what I need."

"Why don't you call him?"

"I don't know his number. He keeps changing it."

"I wonder why." I unlocked the car. "Okay, get in. We'll swing by Del's. You know where it is, right? Or does he keep moving?"

"Pot Luck Alley."

"Oh, good. The classy part of town." We got into my car. "Now I have to figure out exactly why Tori's mad at Nathan," I said.

"Maybe he sided with Elijah against her. Maybe they had a knock down drag out fight."

I started the car, and we drove down the long driveway. "I can't imagine her getting mad at anyone."

"Maybe she and Nathan had an affair. A torrid affair, get it?"

"I get it, but I can't see it. She's so timid."

"Bet she wasn't always timid."

"All right, suppose she and Nathan had a fling. Aaron doesn't sound like the kind of man who'd just give up and leave town." I stopped at the end of the drive. "Pot Luck Alley? Are you sure?"

"So we need some classy music." Jerry turned on the CD of *Tales of Hoffmann*.

I recognized the tune. "This is the I Have Eyeballs song."

"'J'ai des yeux.' Not eyeballs. Eyes."

In the opera, a very strange man gives Hoffmann special glasses so he sees a doll as a living woman. The man has a long song about all the eyes he has, eyes of flame that can see into the depths of the soul, things like that. It's peculiar.

As Jerry hummed along, I wondered again why this opera was the feature presentation. When we first came to Celosia to see the house, he was listening to *Paul Bunyan*. Its themes of once in a blue moon fit perfectly with our new situation: his new house, my new agency. During the Mantis Man case, he listened to *Faust,* its passionate arias underscoring our growing attraction and final declarations of the love we'd always had for each other. But I couldn't make *Tales of Hoffmann* fit. It's his favorite opera, so maybe this meant he was feeling good about life in general.

"What's this part?" I asked.

"'Take them and you will see what you want to. Take my eyes, my living eyes, my eyes of flame, my eyes which pierce the soul, take my eyes.'"

"Okay, I'll take them. Can't Hoffmann figure out this woman is just a mechanical doll?"

"Not until he breaks his glasses."

"So weird."

"His friend tries to tell him, but he won't listen. He's in love."

Take them and you will see what you want to. "I like the next song better."

We drove on to Parkland with Olympia's sparkling "Doll Song" playing. Jerry attempted to sing along, but was overcome with fake coughing as the aria's high notes became too difficult.

"Stick to the Eyeball Song," I said.

DEL'S PLACE IN Pot Luck Alley looked a lot more like a pawnshop than Foster's, dark and cramped. I expected Del to be along the lines of Bilby, but he was a surprisingly tall and handsome man who looked as if he belonged in an upscale clothing store.

"What's up, Jerry? Whatcha need?"

"A gold pocket watch, preferably with an 'S' engraved on it."

"Let me see what I got."

There was just enough room in the corner for a Plexiglas counter, a stool, and a cash register. Every other inch of Del's shop was crammed with appliances, guns, and things I didn't recognize. Del reached into the dark recesses behind the counter and pulled out a faded cardboard box. He put the box on the counter.

"Should be a few in here. Who's the lovely lady?"

"My wife, Madeline. Mac, this is Del Costello."

We shook hands. "A pleasure," Del said. "Are you part of Jerry's scheme?"

"No," I said. "I'm a private investigator."

His eyebrows went up. "Really? We might be able to do each other some favors in the future."

"I'll keep that in mind."

"Too bad you're not in on the game, though. You'd make a stunning distraction."

"Thank you."

"Del," Jerry said. "Wife."

"Force of habit, pal."

The box was filled with pocket watches. Jerry took each one out, examined it, and then set it aside. Most of the watches were made of what looked like tin and were dented and scratched. One that looked as if it were made of bronze fell apart, little springs bouncing everywhere.

"Whoops," Jerry said, trying to retrieve the bits.

Del laughed. "That's okay. I doubt the owner's coming back for that one."

"This all you got?"

"Yep. What about that one?" He pointed to a watch that looked gold, but when Jerry took it out of the box, the gold color came off on his fingers.

"I don't think that one will work."

"That's the only gold one I have. Although, there might be some in another box."

While Del rooted through the mounds of boxes, Jerry took out more watches, each one more pitiful than the last. "This is just junk."

"Well, there's been a run on pocket watches lately. I think some of our acquaintances are shooting for a Jam Auction at the furniture market next month."

"Former acquaintances."

Del paused in his search. "Really?"

"This is my last."

Del gave me a look. "Any particular reason?"

Jerry saw the look. "I've had a good run. I need to get out while I can."

"So you need to go out in style." He blew the dust

off another box and brought it to the counter. "Who's the mark?"

"A couple of women in Celosia."

"Celosia? Slim pickings there, I'll bet."

"I've made a lot of friends."

"Why not tell these women you can't find what they're looking for?"

Jerry looked through the second box. "I may have to."

"Have they paid in deep?"

"I'll be giving their money back anyway."

This was news to me, but I didn't say anything. Del looked equally surprised.

"You're serious?"

"Like I said, I can only push my luck so far."

"So you don't want to hear about the Jam Auction. Or Toby's Charity Raffle?"

"No, thanks."

"Charity Raffle?" I said. "That almost sounds honest."

Jerry took out another sad looking watch and put it back in the box. "Not this one, Mac. Toby gets a big stuffed animal and a roll of tickets. People buy the tickets for a chance at the toy, somebody wins, and all the money goes to charity. Well, maybe a third of the money."

"And I take it a Jam Auction isn't about preserves?"

"Nope. It's a similar scam. Usually involves watches, too. Excess stock. Special Sale. One Day Only."

"On that one, the mark actually ends up buying back his own money," Del said. "It's a thing of beauty. I'd tell you all the details, Madeline, but we have to keep some professional secrets secret."

"That's okay," I said. "If I need the details, I know who to ask."

The search through the second box was just as unsuccessful. Jerry shook his head. "Why is it so hard to find one gold watch?"

Del grinned. "Are these women likely to come after you with a shotgun?"

I thought Flossie Mae might, but not Sylvie. She'd just look at him with sad, disbelieving eyes. Somehow I knew Jerry was trying to avoid that look.

Jerry pushed the box across the counter. "Thanks, Del. Let me give you my number. If you hear of a gold watch, call me."

"One last try, buddy," Del said. "Fred and I are going to play some twinkles at the Pyramid. You sure you don't want in?"

The Pyramid is one of Parkland's fancier gay bars. "Twinkles?" I said. "That doesn't sound very politically correct."

"That's not a term for my people," Del said with a grin. "A twinkle's any reflective surface you can use to see cards. Jewelry works great, and it's not a problem at the Pyramid. Everyone's very festive, especially for the Red Ribbon Ball."

"I wish you every success, Del," Jerry said, "but I no longer twinkle, thank you."

"If you change your mind, it's Saturday night. Great fund raiser for AIDS research."

I waited until we were back in the car before asking my question. "You're giving Flossie Mae and Sylvie their money back?"

"Yes. I'd still like to find a watch, though."

"You know, your reputation as a psychic is no longer at stake."

"I've still got time."

"Anywhere else in Parkland you need to go?"

"No, thanks. I appreciate the detour to Del's. If you turn right here and go down West Avenue until you get to I-40, from there it's about thirty or forty minutes to Rossboro."

Traffic on I-40 was crazy, as usual, but we arrived at the Rossboro exit without being sideswiped or rear-ended. The exit was bristling with signs for every known fast food restaurant. We stopped at Wendy's for drinks and drove on into town, passing many car dealerships, a Wal-Mart, and strip malls filled with tanning salons, video rental stores, and more restaurants. The downtown area looked like a smaller version of Parkland.

"There doesn't seem to be anything special about this place," I said.

"They have a nice park."

"Nice park" was an understatement. In the center of town was a huge park, lush and green with walkways, bike trails, benches, and a large fountain in the center, water splashing from the mouths of smiling stone dolphins. Bordering the park on the far side was a row of antiques shops. On the left was a baseball field and tennis courts. On the right was an amphitheater and a courtyard with tables and chairs.

"This is amazing," I said. "Was all this here when you and Jeff were playing your knife game?"

"It had just been built."

I admired the park and had to admit it looked busy compared to Celosia's calm streets.

"It's not that far away from Celosia if you wanted to open an office here," Jerry said.

"It's something to think about."

"What are we looking for?"

"Clover and Fourth."

"That sign says Third Street."

I turned around the park past Third Street and down the next block to Fourth.

"There's MacDonald's," Jerry said. "Rossboro Baptist Church, Rossboro High School, home of the Fighting Roosters." He chuckled. "Somebody told me they used to be called the Fighting Cocks back in the fifties. He told me this great joke about—"

"Thanks," I said. "We'll just leave it at roosters."

At the corner of Clover and Fourth was a large office building. I found a parking place across the street. We got out, crossed the street, and went inside. Misty May's name was listed on a directory. She was in Suite Fifteen on the fifth floor. We rode the elevator up and found Suite Fifteen. Misty May's secretary, a pleasant-looking older woman, told us she'd let Ms. May know we were here, but things were hectic this afternoon, so she could probably only spare a few minutes.

"We just need a few minutes," I said.

The secretary pressed a button on her phone and said, "Ms. May, Ms. Maclin is here." She smiled. "Go on in."

Misty May was tall and blond. She had on a gray suit and a peach-colored blouse that should have clashed with her coloring, but instead, enhanced her pale good looks. She shook hands with both of us and indicated the chairs in front of her desk.

"Nice to meet you folks. Here's the card. I don't know how it could help you."

The card showed Bufo with his crown, scepter, and smug, "Ha, Ha, I fooled you all" expression. I handed the card to Jerry. "Look familiar?"

"It's the king card."

"Just like the one in Amelia's packs."

"Yes, and in Nathan's."

"It has to mean something."

Misty May shrugged. "I wish I could help you, but I don't know what it means. Elijah just handed it to me. He was laughing, as I said, so he must have thought it was funny. You can have it." She kept looking at Jerry. My husband is the kind of man women look at, but this was a more calculating gaze. "Excuse me, Mister Fairweather, but have we met? You look very familiar."

Jerry didn't even blink. "I was thinking the same thing. Did you go to Parkland High?"

"No, that's not it. I believe I saw you just a few years ago here in town."

Uh-oh, I thought. Was she one of the many people taken in by the knife trick?

Jerry wasn't at all flustered. "You probably saw my brother Tucker. He looks very much like me. He's in a touring company called 'Broadway on the Road.' Did you see Company? He was in the revival."

"That must have been it. I remember it was a show of some kind."

I thought Jerry's lie was very smooth, but I could tell she wasn't completely convinced. I also thought we'd better leave before she figured things out. Fortunately, her secretary called to tell her a client was here.

I stood up and offered my hand. "Thanks so much for your time, Ms. May."

She shook my hand, but she was still looking at Jerry. "Sorry I couldn't help you. You folks have a nice day."

"How much did you take her for?" I asked Jerry as we rode down the elevator.

"You know, it's all a blur."

"A few more minutes, and she would've had you."

"But your timing was great. Didn't you get an adrenaline rush?"

"More like a panic attack."

The elevator doors opened, and we walked out of the building into the bright afternoon sun.

"I just don't have a lot of time," I said. "And I can't forget those paintings I haven't finished."

"You'll make it."

"Do I look that anxious?"

"You have a couple of furrows in your brow, yes."

On the drive home, I wondered what my next move should be. I could talk to more people at the school. I could poke around Nathan's apartment because I had the feeling he knew more than he was telling me. There were many things to consider, not the least of them Jerry.

"Furrows again," Jerry said.

I gave him a look. "I wonder who put them there."

"Jeff and I never used our real names. Misty May will forget all about me."

"How many times have I said that one day your past will catch up with you?"

"When and if it does, I'll deal with it." He turned

on the CD player. A rich baritone voice sang an ominous sounding aria.

"That's foreshadowing if I ever heard it," I said.

"'Scintille, diamante,' as if you didn't know."

I'd heard this aria many times. "Isn't he talking about a sparkly diamond and trapping someone's soul with a mirror? No wonder you love this song."

"Yup. 'The one parts with its life there, and the other loses her soul.'" Jerry sang along for a while. When the aria was over, he turned the music down. "Only I'm not going to lose my soul."

"Good plan."

"I'd keep the sparkly diamond, though."

Traffic was heavy on I-40, so I hadn't really noticed the dark blue Dodge Ram pickup truck until it followed us down the Celosia exit and onto West Avenue. This didn't concern me until it continued to follow my car as I took a couple of short cuts to Main Street. I'd lived in Celosia only a few months, but that was long enough to recognize practically every car in town, and I didn't know this truck.

Relax, I told myself. Why would someone be following you? The only person with a possible grievance was Misty May, and she was not driving the Dodge Ram.

I felt foolish when I pulled into an empty parking place near Deely's Burger World and the truck went past without slowing down. I caught a glimpse of the driver, a large, ordinary-looking bald man who didn't even give me a glance.

Jerry and I went into Deely's and ordered cheeseburgers and fries. We were just digging in when a beefy young man in overalls and a baseball cap pulled low over his narrow dark eyes stopped at our table and glowered at Jerry. He was Jackson Dooley, Sylvie's fiancé.

"Just what the hell is going on with that watch story you been telling Sylvie?"

I had to admire how Jerry didn't flinch. "We're very close to finding it."

"You'd better be. I told her all that fortune telling stuff was crap, and if she was going to marry me, she'd better stop going to your stupid séances and having you tell her all this nonsense about her dead aunts."

"Okay."

Jerry's calm reply wasn't what Jackson expected. I could tell he'd been hoping for a fight. He clenched his fists a few times and looked around the crowded restaurant. He lowered his voice. "So listen up. You'd better come up with a watch, and you'd better tell her that was the last message from dead people. She's all caught up in that spirit stuff, and it's not right. She gets a watch, she's happy, then it's over, and I'm happy, got it?"

"Why don't you get her a watch, then?"

Jackson leaned on the table. "Oh, no. It's gotta come from you, and it better be real, or there's gonna be trouble."

I cleared my throat. Jackson straightened. "Pardon me, ma'am, but he's gotta make it right. He's been leading her on for too long now. I've had enough of his tricks."

I wanted to say, I have, too, but managed to contain myself. "Sylvie and her aunt have enjoyed their visits."

"I'm sure they have, and I'm not saying they can't visit any more, 'cause I can't tell Mrs. Flossie Mae what to do, that's for sure. But they've paid good money, and they deserve results. How long were you planning to string them along, Fairweather?"

"I'll take care of it," Jerry said.

"You damn sure will. I'll give you till Monday. Bright and early." He touched the brim of his cap. "Ma'am."

He lumbered off. I calmly dipped my French fries in ketchup and ate them while Jerry drummed his fingers on the table. Finally he said, "You're not going to say anything?"

"I think Jackson said it all."

"When can we go back to Parkland?"

"Tomorrow."

"That's Thursday."

"That's right."

"That should give me enough time."

"I hope so, or Jackson will be knocking on our door."

"I can take him."

I chuckled. "I can, maybe. I don't know about you."

Jerry stirred his straw around in his Coke. I could tell his thoughts were stirred up, too. "What do you think he'll do?"

"More than likely, he'll punch you in the eye, but I believe his mother works for the *Celosia News*."

Jerry stopped stirring. "Bad publicity for your agency."

"'Fairweather Scams Local Woman' might not be the best thing for Madeline Maclin Investigations."

"It's not going to come to that, Mac."

"You see how these stupid schemes always catch up with you?"

He took a drink. "Well, ordinarily, I'd be long gone by now."

"And you're staying because—?"

"Because now I am a fine upstanding member of the community."

"Who's still holding fake séances."

"I promise I'll hold only one more, hand over the watch, and say good-by to the spirit world."

"Good." I was hunting in my pocketbook for some money to pay the bill when Rachel Sigmon came in with her two daughters. She saw me, waved, and ushered the two girls over to our table.

"Madeline, these are my girls, Bronwen and Magwen. Girls, this is Madeline Maclin, a former Miss Parkland."

As I'd seen in their pictures, Bron and Mag had none of their mother's attractive features. Instead of long dark hair, they had tired brown hair that lay flat on their little round heads. Suspicious eyes gleamed from their doughy little faces. I could only guess they looked like their father.

"Hello, girls. This is my husband, Jerry. Jerry, Rachel Sigmon."

They shook hands. "Nice to meet you, Jerry," Rachel said. "Madeline, I just wanted to tell you the girls are so excited about being in Little Miss Rainbow."

The girls eyed their mother with all the excitement of facing long hours at the dentist.

"For her talent, Bron's playing a piano solo by Edvard Grieg, and Mag is doing a dramatic recitation."

"'The Raven,'" Mag said. "It's a poem."

What cheery choices. "Well, good luck."

"I apologize again for pestering you about coaching them. The director of the pageant said he had plenty of time to show all the girls what to do. Of course they have their dance recital at the theater first. I hope you can stop by the house and visit us some time soon."

"I'll try."

"Okay, girls, let's go. You have a lot of practicing to do. See you later, Madeline."

Bronwen and Magwen sighed and trudged after their mother.

"Poor things," I said.

Jerry grinned. "The Spud Sisters."

I had to laugh. "That's unkind."

"At least their mom isn't after you to coach them any more."

"They would need a lot of coaching. Ready to go?"

"All set."

But next, Fiona Kittering came up. By her tense expression and glittering eyes, I could tell she was a rat terrier on the hunt.

"Madeline, Nathan says you were asking him all sorts of questions about Amelia Lever. What's going on? You can't possibly think he had anything to do with her death, can you?"

"I just wanted to know if he knew her. She was his cousin's fifth grade teacher."

Fiona quivered like a terrier who has caught sight of a squirrel in her territory. "You think he killed Amelia? That's crazy."

"It's my job to ask all kinds of questions. Sometimes the craziest thing can lead to a clue."

"No, it's your job to solve that riddle."

"I'm doing that, too."

The terrier had now jumped off the porch. "But it has to be solved by Monday! Are you any closer to finding the answer? That's why Nathan hired you, not to accuse him of murder."

The people in the next booth were almost leaning over to listen.

"Okay, calm down," I said. "I didn't accuse him of murder. I only asked if he knew Amelia."

"Well, when he called me, he was very upset."

"I'm sorry. I realize he has an important deadline, and that's probably why he's on edge. I'll call and apologize."

Fiona took a deep breath and became human again. "Yes, well, that would be very nice. Sorry I blew up. Guess I've been on edge, too."

"That's all right. You're concerned about him. I understand."

I thought she would say something else, but she turned and left the restaurant.

"Well, that was interesting," I said. "Nathan got upset enough to call her. Was he hoping she'd warn me off? That I'd stop asking inappropriate questions, or give up the case?"

"Okay, so we've both been accosted in Burger World," Jerry said. "What say we go home?"

"That's a very good idea."

WHEN WE GOT HOME, there was a dark blue Dodge Ram pickup truck parked in the driveway.

"Who's that?" Jerry asked.

"I don't know, but the truck followed us from Rossboro."

The man who got out of the truck wasn't just large. He was extra large. He was at least six feet tall, wearing camouflage pants and a tank top. He had more muscles on his arms than Jerry has on his entire body. Even his bald head looked muscular.

He smiled. "Evening, ma'am, sir. Somebody told me this was where the Fairweathers lived. I'm looking for Mister Fairweather."

"That's me," Jerry said.

"I'm Bert Finchner. You owe me five thousand dollars."

I don't know how Bert Finchner managed to look affable and sinister at the same time. Maybe it had something to do with the way he smiled as he loomed over Jerry.

"How do I owe you five thousand dollars, Mister Finchner?"

"Call me Bert. My lady friend, Misty May, called me to say you had stopped by her office, and as luck would have it, I was down at the gas station next to the highway. She recognized you as one of the fellows who had a little knife game going at the fair a couple of years back. Seems she had a bet with some of her girlfriends, and they all gave her some money to bet on the outcome of that game, money I believe you took under false pretenses."

"I'm not sure you can prove that."

Bert Finchner grinned. "Oh, I imagine I can. See, I watch a lot of TV, especially that Discovery Channel. They got a great program called 'How Do They Do That?' Not long after Misty lost her money, they showed on that program how you do that knife trick. Pretty clever, I have to say, but pretty dishonest, too, to take folks' money that way. It's a little set of pegs on the side, and the one the knife's in sticks out just so you can see it, but nobody else can. So you're never gonna slam your hand down on the cup with the knife in it."

I could tell by Jerry's expression that this was exactly how the knife trick was done.

Bert cracked one huge set of knuckles and then the other. "Just give me the money, and I'm outta your way for good. Otherwise, I might have to show you a little knife trick of my own." He smiled at me again. "Begging your pardon, ma'am. I hate to threaten your husband right here in front of you, but he knows what he done. Hope it hasn't scandalized you too much."

"This isn't news to me," I said.

Bert looked surprised. "You part of the act, too?"

"No, I'm trying to reform him."

"Hope that's working for you."

"How do you figure five thousand dollars?" Jerry asked.

"What you took, plus interest."

"I don't have five thousand dollars."

"That's okay. You've got a real pretty wife, who wants the best for you, so here's what I'm gonna do. I'll give you a couple a days to come up with the cash, how's that? What's today, Wednesday?" He counted on his fingers. "Thursday, Friday, Saturday, Sunday— why that's plenty of time. I'll even give you the whole weekend. I'll come back Monday. You don't have it then, I'm calling the law. Fair enough?"

I saw Jerry swallow hard. A gold watch with an "S' and five thousand dollars. Monday was looming large and dark. Just like Bert. "Fair enough."

Bert gave him a slap on the shoulder that almost toppled him over. "Good! I like to settle things nice all around. See you Monday!"

He got into his truck and drove away. Jerry and I stood in the yard for a while.

"I think that was the past," I said, "and I think it just caught up."

FIVE

I WOULD LIKE to say that Jerry and I spent the rest of the night making wild, passionate love, but thanks to Jackson's threat and Bert's unsettling visit, Jerry stayed up watching TV and wandering around. I worked in my studio for a while. Once I got into my painting, something took over, something I couldn't ever explain. I'd paint, then I'd step away, not really knowing how the brush strokes managed to capture the spirit of the leaves, or how the colors blended to make clouds and sky. I really enjoyed bringing the fields and woods to life, carefully overlaying the tones to make depth, copying the scene and yet creating something completely new. I forgot about Amelia Lever and Nathan Fenton, poor little Tori trapped in her house, and the menacing hulk that was Bert Finchner.

I finally went to bed around two. I woke to the sweet smells of cinnamon toast and lay in bed a few more minutes, thinking how lucky I was to have a husband who enjoyed making breakfast.

But this same husband needs a job, I reminded myself. This same husband needs to pay his debts, and I wasn't sure how he could do that. I swung my legs out of bed and plopped my feet firmly on the floor. I had other mysteries to solve first.

I got dressed and combed my hair. When I came into the kitchen, Jerry was at the counter buttering toast.

"How many pieces you want?"

"Two to start, thanks."

I got my coffee and sat down at the table. Jerry put two pieces of cinnamon toast on a plate and brought the plate to me. "Did you get any sleep?" he asked.

"A little. Did you stay up all night?"

He nodded. "I know I said I wasn't going to call Harriet, but this is an emergency."

"What did she say?"

"I called her this morning to see if she could loan me the money. I forgot until I heard her answering machine that she was going with Tucker and Selene to our beach house this week. They won't be back until next weekend. Tucker was my next plan, and he's in Bermuda. They're all in Bermuda."

"I may have enough in my savings account—" I started to say.

"No, this is my mess. I need to clean it up."

"You can pay me back."

"I thought I'd check with some other friends in Parkland."

Was he planning something illegal to pay off Big Bert? "What kind of friends?"

"Scurvy, nasty, pig-stealing friends. We can knock off a couple of banks before lunch."

"Speaking of banks, why don't we see if we can get a loan?"

"This is Thursday. Think they'll approve one today?"

"Not on your credit, but probably on mine. We can stop by and see before we go to Tori's. And some time today I need to visit Rachel and talk to Nathan."

The phone rang. "Maybe Bilby or Del found a

watch," Jerry said. "I'd like one thing to go right today. Hello? Oh, hello, Tori. We were just saying we'd come back to the chateau this morning. Yes, she's here. Hang on." He passed the phone to me.

Tori's voice sounded even more plaintive than usual. "Madeline, I was wondering if you could come over this morning by yourself for a little while."

"Sure," I said.

"I don't want to hurt Jerry's feelings, but I need to talk to you about something."

"It's not a problem."

"He can come later today to continue the search."

"I'm just finishing breakfast," I said. "Then I'll come over."

"Thank you."

She hung up. I handed the phone back to Jerry. "Slight change of plans. Tori needs to talk to me alone this morning. She sounded really down."

"Take her something for her scrapbook. A little sketch, maybe. You got anything that looks like a ballerina up there?"

"No, but it would take only a minute to make one. That's a good idea." I got up. "Come here." I hugged him tight. "We'll work this out."

He grinned and kissed me. "Have you ever thought about making your own hundred dollar bills?"

"Mm, you taste like cinnamon toast. No, and you're not going to, either."

"Well, do you think you could change your plans one more time?"

"Put you at the top of the list, you mean?"

"Just for a few minutes. Then you can go see Tori, Nathan, Rachel, and the rest of Celosia."

ABOUT AN HOUR LATER, I drove up to Chateau Marmot. As usual, Tori was waiting at the door.

"Madeline, thanks so much for coming. I hope I didn't make Jerry angry."

"Not at all." In fact, I'd left Jerry feeling very happy, indeed.

"Well, please come in." She led the way to her dark little parlor. The portrait of Cousin Barnaby leaned against a stack of scrapbooks. "I haven't found out anything else from the picture."

"We'll find the answer, don't worry." I moved a stack of scrapbooks off a chair and sat down. Tori perched in her chair, wringing her little hands. I wanted to cheer her up. "Before we start, I have something for you for your scrapbook." I handed her the little pen and ink sketch I'd done after breakfast and a brief tumble in bed with Jerry. Tori took it in both hands as if it were a holy relic.

"Oh, my goodness. You can't mean for me to have this!"

"I'd love for you to have it."

"It's beautiful! You are so talented."

"Thank you."

"But you can't possibly want to give it up."

"I can draw another."

She clutched it to her. "Thank you so much!"

"I'm glad you like it."

"I'll find a special place for it in my book." She carefully set the drawing aside. "I owe you an explanation."

I waited while she gathered her thoughts.

"Madeline, being in *The Nutcracker* changed my life. Before that, I was just Tori Dewey, the plumber's daughter. After I danced in that ballet, I was someone special. People recognized me. They wanted my autograph. They wanted to take a picture with me. I was finally someone! Madeline, you're a winner. You know how it is."

"Tori, you are someone."

She shook her head. "Not any more."

"What made it change?"

"Aaron. At first, he was proud of me, but then he got tired of everything, all the attention. I think he was a bit jealous. He said what did it matter if I danced in some silly dance? He said ballet was for people who thought they were better than everyone else. But that was exactly what the Fentons and Satterfields thought! It didn't make sense to me, but I loved him, so I said I'd stay at home, go to the club with him, have parties and so on here at the chateau, the whole social scene."

"You gave up your career?"

"Yes. Then one day Aaron said he wanted to leave, and that was that. He said he needed some time by himself."

"I'm so sorry."

"Every day I expect to find divorce papers in the mail. I suppose it will be a relief, in a way. As for Nathan." She paused. "He was interested in me, but I was already engaged to Aaron. I think he might be angry that I married Aaron."

"Have you talked to him about this?"

Tori's little face drooped with sadness. "I tried to once. He said he didn't want to talk to me."

I wasn't sure what to say. With her self-esteem not secure to begin with, this must have been the final blow. "Tori, none of this was your fault."

"Of course, it was. I wasn't woman enough for Aaron, and I tried so hard."

"But if Aaron wasn't really in love with you, you could've been Marilyn Monroe, and he wouldn't have cared."

She wiped away a few tears. "I know. But ever since then, I've been ashamed to go out."

"You shouldn't feel ashamed. Unfortunately, a lot of marriages don't work out."

"I don't know. I thought the whole town was laughing about it."

"Don't you think some people would sympathize with you?"

"It's just so mortifying."

"I'm sorry you had to go through that. Let me change the subject. Why did Elijah let you stay in the chateau?"

She leaned forward. "This was the oddest thing, Madeline. Not long before he died, he came to see me, which scared me to death at first, but he was very polite. He said he may have been wrong about me. He said Aaron had married me to spite him, and he was sorry his nephew had treated me so badly. He said he knew I loved the house and needed a place to stay, and he was going to make sure I could stay here. I must have looked as puzzled as I felt because he told me he knew he was dying and wanted to make some things right. Well, of course, I thanked him. I could hardly believe it."

"And Nathan has no interest in the house?"

"He says he doesn't. Neither does Aaron. I'm very happy to have such a beautiful place, even if it is kind of large."

But it will become your tomb if I can't convince you to get out once in a while. "Tori, I'm going to make a suggestion, and you don't have to say yes or no right now, just think about it. I want you to consider coming to Parkland to see *Sleeping Beauty* with me."

She drew herself in. "Oh, no, I couldn't possibly."

"Just come and be in the audience. I think you'll see that no one will point a finger at you or make some crude remark. In fact, no one in Parkland will know you."

She took my hand in her little hand. "Madeline, I know what you're trying to do, and I appreciate it more than I can say, but I can't leave the house."

"Just think about it."

"I'll think about it, but I already know what my answer will be."

I wasn't sure what else I could say to her. "I'll see you later, then."

This time, she didn't walk with me to the door. She just turned and disappeared into the darkness of her house.

BAD NEWS AT the bank. When I called to ask about a loan, I was informed that I could be approved by Monday. This was cutting things a bit close. I had enough money in my savings account to cover Jerry's debt, but it would put quite a dent in my savings. If Nathan paid the rest of his fee, that would help, but I hadn't solved Nathan's riddle, so I didn't feel I had the right to ask for more money up front.

When I called Jerry to let him know, he said, "Mac, do not take out any of your savings. I told you it was my problem. I'll fix it."

"Yes, but I'm a little worried about your methods."

"Where are you now?"

"I'm on my way to Nathan's. Are you needed at the store?"

"Not until this afternoon."

This made me a little worried, too. "I'll come pick you up. You can go with me."

"Go ahead and detect," he said. "I'm calling in a few favors."

"Jerry."

"And circling the interesting looking want ads in the *Celosia News*. Catch you later."

I sighed as I closed my phone. I had no idea what "calling in a few favors" meant. I didn't want any of Jerry's former partners in crime showing up on my doorstep, but at least he was trying to do something about his situation.

Nathan wasn't home. I called him and got his answering machine. I left a message for him to call me as soon as possible. Then I called Celosia Elementary and asked to speak to Rachel. The secretary told me one of Rachel's daughters wasn't feeling well, and Rachel had taken a sick day to be home with her. I thought maybe I'd gotten another reprieve, but when I called Rachel's house, she said, "Oh, we're fine. Come on over. We'd love to see you."

So I went to Rachel's house.

RACHEL LIVED IN a neighborhood of large split-level homes, all painted green and yellow. I wondered how she knew which one was hers. She was delighted to see me. Both Bronwen and Magwen were watching a Barbie movie on TV and were less than thrilled when their mother switched it off and insisted they sit down at the kitchen table with me.

"I just made a fresh pot of tea, and we have some Girl Scout cookies, if you'd like some."

"Tea will be fine, thanks," I said. "How are you girls?"

"Okay," they said.

"I thought one of you wasn't feeling well today?"

"After their dance rehearsal last night, it took me forever to get them settled, so I let them sleep in this morning," Rachel said. "They were so excited. I told them they did so well. They should be very proud of themselves."

The girls looked bored. Bronwen said, "Mom, can Alex come to my birthday party?"

Rachel frowned. "We'll talk about that later."

"But you promised I could invite anybody I wanted to."

"That's not something we're going to discuss right now."

Bronwen folded her arms and stuck out her bottom lip in a full-blown pout. Magwen grinned. "Bron's got a boyfriend, Bron's got a boyfriend."

"You shut up," Bron said.

Rachel's frown deepened. "Bron! We don't use that expression. Mag, you are not to tease your sister."

"Well, she does."

"Girls, you have a wonderful opportunity to ask Madeline anything you like about being in a pageant, but if the two of you can't behave, you can go up to your rooms."

They sat and looked at me. If I'd been able to read minds, I would have seen a blankness as vast as outer space. Rachel waited, and when she realized her daughters didn't have any questions, or any conversation, she said, "Very well. You're excused from the table. Upstairs. Now."

Bronwen and Magwen did not seem at all concerned about being dismissed. They ran out of the kitchen and up the stairs. Rachel handed me a mug of tea.

"I'm sorry. They're just so wound up. I really appreciate you coming by, though. How's your investigation coming along?"

"Slowly."

"Nothing to indicate Amelia was murdered, I hope."

"I still have some people to talk to."

A muffled crash and an outraged cry from one of the girls sounded overhead.

Rachel got up. "Oh, for heaven's sake. Will you excuse me a moment, please?"

I looked around for someplace to put my tea bag and decided the trash can must be under the sink. In the trash, I saw the familiar metallic gleam of a Bufo card wrapper. There were lots of empty wrappers. Gold wrappers. I looked around, hoping to spy some cards, but Rachel's kitchen was spotless.

I sat back at my place. Rachel returned, looking calm, but there was an edge to her voice. "Madeline, I hope you don't think today is a typical day at my house. Bron insists on having this boy at her party, and he's a seventh grader. Much too old for her. Now she and Mag are quarreling. I think they're over stimulated."

"Maybe they need fewer planned activities."

"Goodness, you should see the mischief they get into if they're not kept on a schedule."

"Are they into the latest fads, like Bufo cards?"

She made a face. "I think those things are a waste of money, but yes, I've gotten them some. Which reminds me, did they ever find out who robbed Georgia's? It was Bobby Berkely, I bet."

"Bobby's still in reform school."

She looked surprised. "Oh, really? Well, he was my best guess. Would you care for some more tea?"

"No, thanks," I said. "I need to go."

"I'm so sorry the girls weren't on their best behavior. Come back when you can stay longer."

I was getting into my car to go to my office when Magwen came dashing around the corner of the house, closely followed by her sister. Magwen was laughing. Bronwen was not. Her little sister was chanting, "Bron's got a boyfriend, Bron's got a boyfriend," and she was so busy looking back to see Bron's reaction, she almost ran into my car.

I caught her arm. "Whoa, hold on."

She regained her balance and doubled her speed. Bronwen, red-faced and panting, stopped and watched her go across the yard. "I told you to shut up, Mag!"

"Take it easy," I said. Neither little girl was in shape for long distance sprints. "Just ignore her. She knows how to get you upset."

"I can invite anyone I like to my party!" Bronwen told her sister.

"They're only coming to see if you really have Bufo cards."

"And I will, too! I'll have a complete set of Bufo cards before anyone else!"

"Did your mother buy you a complete set?" I asked before Magwen could fire her next shot.

Bronwen caught her breath. "She bought me tons and tons of cards so I could get all the best ones."

"Did she buy them at Georgia's books?"

"I don't know."

Magwen had apparently caught her breath, too, and zipped by for another taunt. "Nah, nah, can't catch me."

Bronwen accepted the challenge, and both girls disappeared around the house. That was fine with me. I couldn't do anything about their sibling rivalry. And I wasn't sure I could do anything with the information Bronwen had conveniently supplied.

I HADN'T BEEN IN my office very long before there was a knock on my door, and Shana came in. "Hope I'm not interrupting."

"No, please come in. What's up?"

"Just in town to check on my display at Georgia's." She sat down across from me. "How's your case coming along?"

"Still not much to go on." I had almost forgotten about the little piece of plastic. I took it out of my pocketbook. "Any idea what this is?"

She took it and slowly turned it around. "As a writer I would have to say it looks like the top of a ballpoint pen with the piece that holds the pen to a notebook missing."

"I thought so, too." Something any student might have lost in the grass. I put it back in my pocketbook. "Jerry and I made a little trip to Rossboro."

"Oh, did you like it?"

"Not as much as Celosia, but I might be able to get some work there. We also stopped by to see Elijah Fenton's lawyer, Misty May. Unfortunately, she happens to be a victim of one of Jerry's old scams."

"Oh, dear. What did she say?"

"She sent her giant boyfriend after us. Jerry has a little debt to settle."

"Go to the bookstore right now and tell Georgia you need to have a talk with your husband."

"He says he's taking care of it."

"Well, I hope so. How's the riddle coming along?"

"We think the line about animals living in packs refers to Bufo cards."

She laughed. "It would be just like Elijah to throw a curve like that. Can you and Jerry come to dinner tonight?"

"Thanks, but we've got several things to do in Parkland today. We'll probably eat there."

"The drive to Parkland will be an excellent opportunity for a discussion with your husband. If you don't like what he says, you can leave him by the side of the road."

"Which is exactly where he might want to be. Ms. May's boyfriend is pretty huge. And Sylvie's fiancé isn't too happy with Jerry, either. He gave Jerry until Monday to come up with the pocket watch from Beyond."

"This has to do with the séances, right?"

"It's something he's promised Sylvie and Flossie Mae. I'd be more concerned except these threats are probably going to make an honest man out of him. He actually said something about giving all their money back."

She chuckled. "What about your art work, Madeline? Are you ready for the Weyland Gallery?"

"Almost."

"Are you excited? It really is a great opportunity."

"Yes, it is." And it may heal the rift between my mother and me, I wanted to add, but I thought I'd better wait and see if that really happened. "A great opportunity for a lot of reasons."

"Well, Hayden and I will be there."

"Thanks." And I hope to introduce you to my mother.

BESIDES HIS DEBTS, I had other things I needed to discuss with Jerry. As soon as he finished with a customer, I told him about finding gold wrappers in Rachel's trash can.

"Do you remember selling any cards to her?"

"No. She could've bought them in Parkland. Didn't you say her girls went to school there?"

"You're probably right."

"Well, speaking of cards, I may have something," he said. He reached behind the counter and brought out a box of Bufo cards. "These are the cards that were in Amelia's and Nathan's packs. I've had plenty of time to examine them today. The king cards say, 'King of All Four Corners of the World,' so I decided to look in the corners." He put several cards on the counter. "Check it out."

At first, I couldn't see anything. The edges of the cards were decorated with elaborate scrolls and stylized plant leaves and stems. "Wait a minute. Is that a 'C'?"

"Yep."

Hidden in the designs were small green letters. "Do all the cards have these?"

"That's the tricky part. Only a few in each pack have

letters in the corners, but my guess is Elijah picked out
the ones he wanted to spell a clue."

I squinted and found an "A" amidst the coiling vines.
"Then he scattered them in several packs and resealed
them. This is great, Jerry, but have you figured out what
the letters spell?"

"So far, I've only been able to find a 'C' and an 'A.'
It's eye-crossing work."

"This would explain why the thief took all the packs
from the store, but how did he know the cards held a
clue?"

"Somebody else is on to Elijah's game."

I nodded. "Somebody who may have tried to get into
Aaron's house, not knowing he threw his cards away."
I took out my phone and called Aaron's number. This
time I got an answering machine that informed me Mr.
Satterfield was out of the office. I left a message for
him to call me and hung up.

"Are we heading to Parkland?" Jerry asked.

"Yes. Nathan's not home. I'll talk to him when we
get back."

Jerry put the cards back in the box. "Okay. I get to
drive this time. You can have a go at finding letters."

I waited to voice my concerns until we were turning
off Main Street onto the road leading down the highway that runs from Celosia to Parkland. "Exactly what
did you mean by calling in some favors?"

He took a moment and then grinned. "Can't keep
anything from Madeline Maclin, Ace Detective."

"Seriously, Jerry, if your questionable friends are
going to descend on Celosia, I want to be prepared."

"I wouldn't call them questionable. Sleazy, maybe."

"Just tell me what's going on."

"It's okay. I called a few old pals and explained about Big Bert. I'm hoping they can wire me some cash before Monday."

"Really? They said they'd help you out?"

"They're sleazy, not heartless. And we go way back."

"Well, that's a relief."

"If they come through for me. How did Tori like her picture?"

"She loved it. I keep trying to convince her to come with us to the ballet in Parkland. She's afraid people will laugh at her because her husband left her."

"Wish we could find that guy. I'd like to set Bert on him."

By the time we got to Parkland, I'd managed to find an "I" in the corner of another card.

"'CIA,'" Jerry said. "Great. Now we've got the government involved."

We stopped by Bilby Foster's pawnshop first where Jerry got the bad news that a gold watch with an "S" engraved on it would not be available until Saturday.

"Best I can do," Bilby said. "Thought you was out of the game."

"This is different and very important."

"Well, you can try Royalle's. Cost you the earth, though. Most of the better jewelry stores are going to be expensive."

"Did you try Jack?"

"Jack's in jail. You go by Del's?"

"No luck there. What about Morey?"

"Haven't seen him."

Jerry thanked him and said he'd be back on Saturday. We got in the car. Jerry slumped in his seat. "Why is it so hard to find one little watch?"

"Would a trip to Baxter's Barbecue cheer you up?" I asked.

"Only if you're paying."

Baxter's Barbecue is our favorite place to eat in Parkland. The décor isn't fancy, but the food is amazingly good. Even the smells are deliciously fattening. The owners waved from behind the counter, and almost before we'd taken our seats, we had paper plates full of plump barbecue sandwiches oozing with rich sauce and crispy fries in front of us, along with a red plastic basket of hushpuppies and two large Cokes.

Jerry took a bite of his sandwich, chewed and said, "Ahh, I don't care how bad life gets, it can all be cured with one bite of Baxter's barbecue. I'll die full and happy."

"I doubt Jackson will kill you."

"Maybe I could set Jackson and Bert against each other. I'd actually pay to see that." He put on an announcer's voice. "Redneck Rumble! Sunday, Sunday, Sunday!" He switched back to his normal voice. "That would take care of both my problems."

"Only they both happen to be in the right."

"Yeah, but I don't like the idea that Jackson's relatives down at the *Celosia News* could mess with your career."

I sighed. "Things are not going too well, anyway."

"Give Warwick a call. If he doesn't have anything for you, we won't have to go over there."

"Excellent idea."

Warwick sounded apologetic. "Not much news,

Madeline. Mrs. Lever had a heart condition, and the doctor I spoke with said she had a heart attack."

"So it didn't have anything to do with the nicotine patch?"

"No, sorry."

I remembered the bottle of pills I'd found in her bag. "What about K-Dur? Could her prescription have been tampered with? Could she have died of an overdose?"

"Well, here's the problem. K-Dur's a brand of potassium, and if Mrs. Lever took too much, it could cause an abnormal rhythm and possibly a heart attack. But when someone dies, the cells release potassium, so it's impossible to tell if there was an overdose. If someone wanted to kill her with an overdose of potassium, they would have to inject it into a vein."

"Did the doctors check for needle marks?"

"Since there was no reason to suspect foul play, there wasn't an autopsy. There were some circular marks on Mrs. Lever's arm, however. When I asked about that, the doctor said she had a skin condition."

"Circular marks?"

"About the size of a quarter."

"They weren't from the nicotine patch?"

"No, the ones she used were square-shaped."

"Hang on a second, Milton." I spoke to Jerry. "Warwick says his contact at the hospital told him Amelia's death is being ruled a heart attack. But he also mentioned the doctors found some odd circular marks on her arm. Circles about the size of a quarter. Remind you of anything?"

Jerry laughed and almost choked on his fries. "Deadly Bufo stickers?"

I handed him another napkin. "I have to consider any clue, no matter how crazy."

"Mac, I can't see Amelia Lever opening a pack of Bufo cards and slapping the stickers on. And if they were deadly, then you'd have kids falling down everywhere, wouldn't you? We found those things all over the school."

"Not if the killer had a special pack made just for Amelia."

"Potassium-laced Bufo stickers?"

"I just happen to have some stickers I found in Amelia's bag. We can take these stickers to Warwick and see if they're toxic."

"Just ask him."

I spoke into my phone. "Is it possible to put potassium on stickers and have it absorb through the skin?"

"No. You'd have to inject someone."

"Not change their pills?"

"Most potassium pills are huge, Madeline. I think someone would notice."

"Does potassium come in a liquid prescription?"

"Yes, but to get the kind that's injected, you'd have to have access through a hospital. Usually emergency rooms have some on their crash carts. Are you thinking about those toad stickers? Not a possibility."

"Okay, thanks. You've been a great help. I appreciate it."

"Always here for you."

I put my phone away and attacked my sandwich. "Another theory shot down in flames."

"At least we don't have to worry about Austin putting deadly stickers all over himself. But I have to admit potassium-laced Bufo stickers sounded so cool."

I enjoyed a few bites of my sandwich and then managed to set it down on the plate. Maneuvering a fat Baxter's barbecue sandwich is always a challenge. "If Amelia was murdered, someone had to get close enough to inject her. The only people on the loading dock were Rachel and Jacey, the cafeteria worker."

"Maybe Amelia had a visitor right before she went out for a smoke."

"We still don't know if she was murdered, just that everyone wanted her dead. And who stands to gain from her death? She didn't leave a vast fortune like Elijah Fenton. I'm going to have to tell Thad Murphy his school's reputation is safe. There goes my paycheck and possibly your nose."

"That's okay," Jerry said. "My huge bookstore salary can pay the bills."

We sat for a while. My appetite was gone. Jerry chewed half-heartedly on his last French fry. "We don't seem to be having any luck, do we?"

"As soon as we solve the riddle, I'll get right back to work on the paintings. Maybe I'll sell all three."

"Don't sell 'Blue Moon Garden.'"

"I will if it'll keep you from losing valuable parts."

"It's the best thing you've ever done," he said. "And don't give up on Amelia. If you feel something's wrong, then you need to solve her murder—although I draw the line at digging her up to look for needle marks."

"I'm glad to know you have limits. Besides, she was cremated."

"There went the evidence. By the way, my limits do not include French fries. How about another round?"

While Jerry worked his way through another order of fries, I took out the Bufo cards and continued the

letter search. "Maybe these three letters are an abbre-
viation or code for something else. Or maybe they don't
mean anything. Oh! Here's a 'T'!"

"If we find a 'Y,' we could spell 'A CITY,'" Jerry
said.

"Not much help. And we don't have a 'Y.'" I took
my pen from my pocketbook and began to jot down
combinations on my napkin. "'CIAT,' 'TAIC,' 'ACTI.'
I'm just getting nonsense words."

"We need more letters." Jerry set his plate aside and
reached for another handful of cards. We stared at the
flourishes and curlicues until I was almost dizzy. After
a while, he said, "There's another 'T,' but I don't know
if it belongs with the other letters, or Elijah goofed.
Now we can spell 'CATTI.'"

"No," I said with sudden excitement. "Now we can
spell 'ATTIC.'"

"Is there an attic in the chateau?"

"I'll bet there is. Let me call Tori."

Tori answered on the first ring. I had an image of
her sitting by the phone, hoping someone would call.

"Yes, there's an attic."

"Jerry and I would like to check it out," I said.

"Of course!"

"We're in Parkland right now. I'll call you when
we get back to Celosia." I hung up and called Nathan.

This time, he answered, and I said, "We may have
a good clue to the riddle. Can you meet us at the chateau, say, in about an hour?"

"That's great, Madeline," he said. "But I'm out at the
camp right now. Why don't you come have a look? Just
take Route Sixteen up to Chandler Road and make a

right. You'll see signs for the camp. Then make a right on Camp Lakenwood Trail."

"Okay," I said. I closed my phone. "I've finally made contact with Nathan."

"You look a little puzzled. Didn't he say, 'Hooray! The riddle's almost solved! I'll meet you at the chateau'?"

"No. We're off to Camp Lakenwood."

WE DROVE BACK TO Celosia, found Camp Lakenwood Trail, and drove down a twisting gravel road through the woods until we reached a wooden rail fence. The gate was open. We drove under an archway carved with the words: "Camp Lakenwood, Established 1954."

"I wish it had a better name," Jerry said. "Like Camp Wahchahooche or Camp Webelongen."

"Maybe Nathan will take one of your excellent suggestions. Did the Fairweather boys ever camp?"

"Just in the back yard. However, I've slept in the woods many times."

"I don't think running from the law counts as camping."

The road stopped at a small parking lot. We parked next to an ancient school bus that had been painted green with "Camp Lakenwood" in yellow letters on the side and got out. A yellow sign shaped like a lopsided arrow pointed toward a large log cabin. The sign said, "Welcome!" in faded green letters. Fallen branches and clumps of pine needles cluttered the pathway.

"Camp Novideo," Jerry said. "Camp Bennforgotten."

Nathan met us at the door of the log cabin. In his khaki shorts and green and yellow Camp Lakenwood tee shirt, he looked alert and full of energy, a direct

contrast to the anxious, flustered man trying to orga-
nize mounds of paperwork.

"Welcome to Camp Lakenwood! What's all this
about a clue to the riddle?"

"We need to have a look in the chateau's attic," I
said. "I thought you might like to come along."

"Well, yes, sure, but I'm really glad you could come
see the camp. Let me give you a quick tour."

He was so excited, I knew I'd have to wait until we'd
seen every inch of the camp.

"Come on in. This large cabin is the office and
where the counselors sleep."

The office, unlike Nathan's apartment, was neatly
organized. Besides the office, there was a large room
with sofas and chairs placed in front of a fireplace. The
furniture was covered in designs of bear and deer. A
large tree stump served as the base for a table made of
pine planks, and the walls were covered with plaques,
banners, and antlers.

"Nice and rustic," Jerry said.

Nathan beamed. "I know. It's perfect. We'll just go
out the back door." We followed him out. "And over
here we have the cabins for the kids."

On the other side of the large log cabin was a clearing of hard packed earth. In the center of the clearing
was a huge ring of white stones encircling a pile of
charred logs.

Nathan eyes were shining. "Here's where we had
our camp-fire every night with stories and songs. Some
of the world's best ghost stories were told around this
campfire, and don't get me started on the songs. Great
songs, really hilarious. Let me show you one of the
kids' cabins."

Surrounding the clearing were smaller cabins, all made of dark wood. Inside the cabins were bunk beds and little tables and chairs. Everything looked worn and smelled musty. Cobwebs had taken over most of the corners.

"Of course, I'll replace all this with new stuff," Nathan said. "And it wouldn't be Camp Lakenwood without the lake."

He led us down a slight hill to a wide blue lake sparkling in the sun. A few leaves had started to change, and the bright bursts of red and yellow reflected in the water. Rowboats sat upside down on the bank, their hulls cracked and full of holes. Faded canoes were stacked on the dock, which was missing several planks and leaned dangerously to the left.

"All the canoes and boats will have to be replaced, as well, and I want to have some small sailboats and maybe some wave runners." He pointed across the lake. "On the other side are some Indian teepees that were made in the fifties, and an obstacle course, and a couple of tree houses that are falling apart."

He stood for a moment looking out across the lake. I knew he was seeing his camp restored and children, all in green and yellow tee shirts, playing in the water, rowing canoes to the other side to explore the teepees and tree houses. I exchanged a glance with Jerry.

"Everybody's got a dream," he said. "Might as well dream big."

I knew he was talking about me, but Nathan said, "Exactly. Why not? Now, let me show you the crafts building."

We passed some weathered picnic tables and a sad-looking basketball court with the remains of nets dangling on the goals on our way to another log cabin. This cabin had a long room furnished with tables and benches.

Nathan indicated the cabinets along the walls. "All the craft supplies are gone, stolen, I'm afraid. Parts of the rail fence are missing, too, but overall, the buildings are sound. I definitely want to install some sort of security system. You see I've got a lot to do."

"It's a beautiful place, though," I said.

"Oh, yes, especially in the fall. I'd love to have sessions starting in the spring and running all the way through October."

We came back out and stood looking across the lake. I still couldn't understand why he wasn't racing back to the chateau to search the attic. My cell phone rang. I checked the caller ID and saw it was Aaron's number.

"Excuse me, Nathan." I answered the phone, and the secretary said, "I'm sorry, Ms. Maclin, but Mr. Satterfield will be out of the office the rest of the day. Perhaps I can help you."

"Thank you," I said. "I want to make an appointment to see Mr. Satterfield tomorrow, if possible."

"I'm afraid Mr. Satterfield won't be available until Monday," she said. "He's on the planning committee for the Red Ribbon Ball, which is Saturday, and he'll be making arrangements for that all day tomorrow. I can make an appointment for you for Monday, if that works for you."

"I didn't realize he was involved with the Red Ribbon Ball," I said, as Jerry's eyes widened. "That's a fund raiser for AIDS, isn't it?"

"Yes, one of the biggest in the city. Mr. Satterfield

always takes an active part in these events. He lost his partner to AIDS last year."

"I'm very sorry to hear that," I said. "I hope the ball is a big success. I'll get back to you about an appointment, thanks." I hung up. Jerry's eyes were still wide. "Aaron's on the planning committee for the Red Ribbon Ball. His partner died of AIDS last year."

Nathan looked pale. "His partner?"

"Yes. So I imagine Aaron is gay. Did you know?"

"N-no, I knew he left town to start a business with a friend, but I never—there was no indication—I mean, he was always doing all sorts of sports and outdoor things." His voice trailed off. "I don't mean that the way it sounds."

A lot of things were making sense to me. "If you didn't know, then I'm sure Tori doesn't know," I said. "I would think Aaron feels guilty for marrying her in the first place and then realizing he had feelings for his friend."

"But he insisted on marrying her," Nathan said.

"Yes, to spite Elijah. I seriously doubt Aaron could have told Elijah he was gay, and being married to Tori was a good cover for a while."

Nathan looked as if he were beginning to understand. "He always seemed so angry."

"So he finally left town and started a new life in Parkland." I thought of something else. "And that's why he doesn't want to be involved in Elijah's treasure hunt. He'd have to come back to Celosia and face a lot of things he doesn't want to face."

"I really didn't know," Nathan said.

"Okay, I'll grant you that," I said, "but it would help if you'd be honest with me about a few other things."

"What? When have I not been honest?"

"Well, for one thing, Amelia Lever was helping you with the grant."

He went pale. "Why do you say that?"

"I found a copy of the grant among her things. She'd written a note that said, 'Nathan, you need to check this.' And she was at your house a couple of days before she died, wasn't she?" As he stammered for a reply, I said, "I found her cigarettes in the ashtray. Convince me you wear purple lipstick, and I'll apologize."

Nathan gulped, but didn't say anything.

"From what I know about Amelia, she loved to ruin plans, especially plans with grants attached. Was she trying to ruin your plans?"

"It's not like that."

"Then what's it like?"

"It's complicated." .

"If you want me to help you, you need to tell me everything."

"I need the answer to that riddle."

"And I need to know why I shouldn't figure you killed Amelia Lever."

He almost fell over. "What? You can't say that!"

"Why not? She was in your house a few days before she died. Maybe the two of you quarreled over the grant money. Maybe she threatened you, and you decided to get rid of her."

"No, no. Please. Let me explain."

Nathan sighed and sat down on one of the picnic table benches. He took off his glasses and rubbed his nose. Then he took some deep breaths as if gathering his courage.

"I told you Aaron was in Mrs. Lever's fifth grade.

Every now and then, Amelia would have a favorite student. Aaron happened to be one of those fortunate few. After he left school, she kept in touch with him. When he left town, occasionally she'd call me or come over to talk about him. She was a gruff old bird, but I got to like her. She knew about Elijah's riddle. She kept telling me to be careful and not let anyone else know about it."

"I think everyone in town knows about it."

"They might know there's a riddle, but not exactly what it says."

"Fiona knows."

"Yes, but I trust her. Amelia was concerned that someone else might find out."

"From what I've learned about Amelia, her concern for you is somewhat out of character."

"She liked me. She said I was one of the few people she could talk to. Really all I did was listen. She was worried about her sons marrying the wrong women. She was angry about how things were run at school. She hated giving the students those endless tests. A few days before she died, she came over to visit. You're right. She was helping me with the grant. She said I needed to be extra careful because she thought someone was going to get my money."

"Did she say who she suspected?"

"No. I told her not to worry. I'd soon solve the riddle."

"Who else knows about this?"

"I don't know. I didn't tell anyone."

"Does anyone else want this camp? Wouldn't the land be valuable?"

"I can't think of anyone else who's shown any interest in it."

"Okay," I said. "One more question. Why don't you want to go back to the chateau?"

He gulped and looked down at his shoes. "It's Tori."

"Do you still have feelings for her?"

"I wanted to take our friendship to the next level, but Aaron was there, and she chose him instead."

"Did she know how you felt?"

"I got angry with her. I told her she was making a huge mistake. Then after I learned how Aaron had treated her, I realized he probably forced her into marriage. He's always been very assertive. I could've helped her, but I didn't. Now she doesn't want to talk to me."

Knowing how sensitive Tori was, I could understand her confusion. "But she's helping us search. She wants you to succeed."

"That's sweet of her, but I know she still hates me."

"She's upset because Aaron left her. She thinks everyone in Celosia is laughing at her."

"I'm very sorry she feels that way. It's not true."

"Well, don't tell me, tell her. She needs to know the truth. Come with us to the chateau."

He looked out across the lake. I figured he was thinking he'd do anything for a chance to own Camp Lakenwood. Then he looked back at me. "All right," he said.

NATHAN HAD A FEW things to do before he left the camp, so Jerry and I went on to the chateau. I was anxious to talk to Tori. I wasn't sure how she'd take the news. As we drove up and parked in front of the house, I realized that Elijah had known exactly what he was doing when he left Chateau Marmot to Tori. If the answer to the riddle was in the attic, neither Aaron nor Nathan would have much chance of getting in, and Tori certainly wouldn't have opened the door to Amelia Lever.

Tori was delighted, as always, to see us. We sat down in her dark little parlor and I explained that Nathan felt very bad about his past behavior and was concerned that she was still angry with him.

"Dear me," she said, twisting her little hands in her lap. "I really don't know how I feel about that. I suppose that makes me feel a little better. It won't do any good to be angry, will it?"

"And there's something else you need to know," I said. "It's about Aaron. Remember I said that if Aaron wasn't in love with you, you could've been Marilyn Monroe, and he wouldn't have cared?" She nodded. "Well, that's more accurate than we thought. He's gay, Tori."

She stared at me. "What?"

"I know he married you to spite Elijah, but then he realized he'd made an even bigger mistake and didn't know how to tell you. Instead of explaining, he just left."

She looked confused. "So there wasn't another woman?"

"No. When he left Celosia with a friend, that friend was a man. They were partners."

She gave a little laugh that was almost a sob. "Really?"

"I know this is upsetting, but I hope it explains things."

She took a shaky breath. "Well, that explains the money."

"What money?"

"Aaron sends me money every month. We're not divorced, so he doesn't have to send alimony. Now I know why he does this. It's his way of saying I'm sorry." She began to cry.

Jerry quickly gave her his handkerchief, and she wiped her eyes. She took another breath. "I guess he still cares for me."

"I'm sure he does," I said, even though I wasn't so sure. Being married to Tori had kept Celosia's nosier citizens—and Elijah—from discovering Aaron's secret. If he felt any emotion, it was probably guilt.

Tori patted her cheeks dry. "How did you find out, Madeline?"

"His secretary told me Aaron was in charge of the Red Ribbon Ball, which is a fund raiser for AIDS and that Aaron's partner died last year."

"Oh, no. How sad!" Her eyes filled with tears again. "All this must have been so hard on him."

I couldn't be as sympathetic, but I could tell Tori was finding a way to cope with the unsettling news. "I imagine he has a lot of friends in Parkland to help him out."

"You're right. That's why he moved there, to be with his friends." She gave her eyes one last wipe. "And I have my friends here. Let's work on solving that riddle."

"Nathan would like to come over and help look, if that's all right with you."

She nodded. "Yes, that's fine."

"He's on his way from Camp Lakenwood. Why don't we wait outside?"

I thought Tori might object, but she went with me and Jerry as we stepped out her front door into the beautiful afternoon. She squinted and held her hand up to shield her eyes.

"My, that sun is bright."

How many years has it been since you were out in the sun? I wanted to ask. I tried to be more tactful. "Do you look after the plants?"

"Oh, I do a little gardening in the back," she said.

I wasn't sure I believed that. I wondered if the back garden looked as sad and neglected as the front. We sat down on the low stone wall. Tori eyed the driveway and twisted her hands nervously.

"Are you okay with this?" I asked.

"Yes. He really should be a part of the search."

"Are you okay with everything, though?"

"I'm all right," she said. "Thank you for telling me, Madeline. I guess I was wrong about a lot of things."

"You just didn't have all the information. That happens sometimes."

She managed a wan smile. "My mother used to say a little learning is a dangerous thing. I should have been more assertive. I should have asked questions."

After a long pause, Jerry said, "I wish Nathan would get here. I'm ready to climb up in the attic. I hope it's spooky and full of bats and cobwebs."

Tori brightened. "It is!"

He gave her a skeptical look. "And how many times have you climbed up in the attic?"

She gave him an impish smile. "I've been up there lots of times."

"No, you haven't. What for? Is the whole attic filled with scrapbooks?"

"Not yet."

By the time Nathan arrived, Jerry's teasing had Tori

feeling more relaxed. Nathan's sincere apology helped, too. He still had on his camp tee shirt and shorts, so he looked like an earnest Boy Scout. He took her hand.

"Tori, I'm so sorry there's been this misunderstanding between us. I was angry because you chose Aaron instead of me, and then I never did anything to help you. You have every right to keep me out of the house. Elijah did one good thing in his life when he left it to you."

I wasn't sure she was going to answer him, but after an awkward moment, she said, "I did like you very much, Nathan, but unfortunately for me, I fell in love with Aaron. I didn't know he wanted to marry me to spite Elijah. I didn't know he was gay. It must have been very hard for him."

"I should've known that. I should've told you."

"Well, you didn't know, either. I shouldn't have blamed you."

"I'm so sorry, Tori."

She managed a smile.

"It's all right," she said. "I actually feel a little better. If Aaron was in love with a man, then I couldn't have done anything to change that, could I? For years, I imagined him with another more beautiful, more talented woman. This is so different I really can't say I feel too badly about it. Let's forget the past and start over by solving your riddle."

With Jerry and Nathan's help, we managed to pull down the rusty chains that held the steps to the attic. The attic stretched into darkness, cobwebs trembling in the slight breeze from the door. Tori flipped a light switch, and the faint glow from dim light bulbs revealed dusty floorboards, a few old trunks, and rows of dark portraits leaning against the walls. The Fentons and the Satterfields were not attractive people, but must have been vain, because it looked as if every single person ever born to these families had a portrait.

"Okay, let's start at one end and work our way down," Jerry said.

He pulled the first one out and brought it closer to the best source of light. We examined it from all sides, found nothing, and he took it back. Then Nathan brought the next one over. We saw Fentons and Satterfields in dark brocade jackets and high heeled shoes of the 1700s, in dark empire waist gowns and cropped curls of the 1800s, and in dark high-necked dresses and dark wool suits of the early 1900s.

Jerry hauled the next portrait up to the light. "When was color invented?"

"They are a grim bunch," I said.

"I love their names. Determination Fenton. Heathcliff Satterfield. Retribution Fenton. Here's a happy soul named Somber. Somber Satterfield. Try saying that fast."

Tori peered at the next serious face. "I guess life was much harder then."

"But if life was hard, wouldn't you like to be called something cheerful, like Hope, or Giggles? Giggles Satterfield. I'd pay to see a portrait of her."

Tori got the giggles, herself. "I don't think that's likely, do you?"

"Not in this attic."

I looked at Somber Satterfield, checked the frame and the back, and slid the portrait over to Jerry. "Next, please."

He leaned Somber against the wall and pulled the

next portrait over. "Let's see what this guy's name is. 'Constant Lyes.' Well, his folks thought a lot about him."

"'Lyes'?" I said, and we all realized what we'd found.

"'And listen where the portrait lies'!" Nathan said. "Maybe this is it."

"Is there a sparrow?" Tori asked. "And a river?"

"It's hard to see."

"'Take heed to see what can't be seen,'" Tori said. "It all fits!"

"Let's get it closer to the door."

Jerry carried the portrait to the attic door. In better light, we could see Constant Lyes Fenton, as dark and grim as Cousin Barnaby and all the other Fentons, standing in a typical portrait pose, one arm outstretched, the other tucked in the front of his jacket. A small stream was in the background, along with some trees and muddy clouds. At the end of his outstretched hand was a small brown bird, just about to light on his fingers.

Tori grasped my arm with both her hands. "Oh, my goodness! This has to be it!"

We turned the portrait over and felt along the back. "There's something here," I said. I borrowed Jerry's pocketknife and made a small slit in the back. I pulled out an envelope. Jerry set the portrait aside. We sat down at the attic entrance. I handed the envelope to Nathan, and he opened it. Inside was a letter and yet another Bufo card. This one showed Bufo holding his Power Stone above his head in triumph, gold rays shining in all directions.

Nathan read the letter aloud, his voice trembling. "'If you are reading this, congratulations. Take this key to my attorney, Misty May, in Rossboro. Use your money wisely.'"

A small key was taped to the letter.

"The one true key!" Tori said. She clapped her little hands. "We did it! We solved the mystery."

"I can't believe it," Nathan said.

I checked my watch. "You have time to get to Rossboro. Give Misty May a call and tell her you're on your way."

He nodded. "Come with me, Tori."

"Oh, no," she said. "I'd better not."

"How about you, Madeline? Jerry? I'm so excited, I'm not sure I can drive."

"I'll be happy to take you," I said, "but Jerry better stay here."

Jerry helped Tori down the attic steps. He and Nathan pushed the steps back up into the ceiling. Tori dusted her hands. "Well, I guess this is good-by," she said.

"You're sure you won't come with me?" Nathan asked. "I never would have found the key without your help."

"No, thank you," she said. "I'm glad we're friends again, though."

"And it's not good-by," I said. "We'll come visit again. I may need your help with some other cases."

"That's really sweet of you, Madeline."

"And I promised to teach you some magic tricks," Jerry said.

I could see she was pleased by our offers, so I made one last try. "And Tori, Jerry and I would still like you to come with us to the ballet. You know now nobody will be talking about you and what happened with Aaron."

"I don't know. Parkland is a long way off."

"Thirty minutes, that's all."

She smiled. "I'll think about it, Madeline. Now hurry and get Nathan's inheritance! I can't wait to hear what happens!"

Nathan called Misty May, who told him she'd be glad to wait until he got to her office. He was so nervous he agreed to let me drive his car to Rossboro.

When he handed Misty May the key and Elijah's letter, his hand shook so badly, he almost dropped both items.

"It's okay, Mr. Fenton," she said. "This is the right key." She opened a small safe in her office and took out a stack of important looking papers. "These bearer bonds belong to you now. I think you'll find that over the years, they've increased in value. I believe the total is close to three million dollars."

"That's a lot of bat houses," I said.

Once Nathan had recovered from that shock, he signed the proper papers, and Misty May's secretary and I signed as witnesses that the bonds were handed over to a legitimate participant in the riddle game. Misty May put them in a briefcase and cautioned Nathan to put his winnings in a safe deposit box right away.

"I intend to," he said.

"The bank's our next stop," I said. "I have business there, too."

She gave me a keen stare. "I would imagine so."

At the Celosia National Bank, while Nathan deposited his money, I took mine out. I didn't care if Jerry would protest. I had enough to cover his debt. I'd just have to find more cases. Nathan would certainly give me a glowing recommendation.

"I can't thank you enough, Madeline," he said. "This has been quite an experience."

"I hope you have the money you need to fix up the camp," I said.

"Oh, yes. It's going to be the best camp ever. And I'm going to frame this Bufo card."

Nathan drove us back to Celosia. On the way, I called Tori to tell her the good news, and then called Jerry to tell him I was on my way home. Nathan dropped me off and waved at Jerry as he drove away.

"Did you have to go a few rounds with Misty May?" Jerry asked me.

"That's taken care of." As I'd predicted, he was not happy to hear I'd taken money out of my savings account to pay off Big Bert.

"Mac, I told you not to do that."

"Have you heard from any of your friends?"

"Well, no."

"Then we'll give this money to Mr. Finchner on Monday, and you can start paying me back."

"I will pay back every cent, I promise."

I gave him a kiss. "I know you will."

"The riddle's solved," Jerry said. "What's next?"

"I'm going to work in my studio for a while, that's what's next."

SIX

I HAD TIME to finish the landscape that evening. Then I worked most of Friday morning on the third picture, keeping an eye on the time. I wanted to go by Celosia Elementary after the children had gone, but before the school closed for the day.

Jerry wanted to come along. "What do you want to do?" he asked as we went out to the car.

"I need to find out if anyone else on the faculty has a condition that requires a syringe. I suppose the secretary might have that information." Wait a minute. Someone else at the school would have that information, and access to syringes. I stopped so suddenly, Jerry ran into me.

"Whoa," he said. "What did you think of?"

"School nurse, Brenda Mullins. She probably has everyone's medical records, and she would have access to anything at the hospital, including potassium."

"But didn't you tell me she's something of a dim bulb? And she was at the high school when Amelia died."

"I'll admit she seems an unlikely suspect, but she may have provided the killer with what he or she needed."

BRENDA MULLINS LOOKED at Jerry and me with wide eyes. "I can't give you that information. Personal health records are not for public view."

"I'd just like to know if anyone on the faculty has diabetes or a health condition that requires them to take shots."

"I'm the only one who's supposed to give shots."

"I understand that. Could you tell me if anyone on the faculty knows how to administer shots?"

"I'm sure I don't know. They're not supposed to, so why would they?"

"There aren't any students who require help with injections?"

"I can't tell you that."

By the time we got to the school, everyone had left for the day except Thad Murphy, the secretary, and fortunately, Brenda Mullins. The school's first aid room was about the size of a closet, so Jerry was standing behind her. He pantomimed wringing her neck.

"Do you also work at the hospital, Ms. Mullins?" I asked, thinking, I hope I never have you as my nurse.

"No, I'm strictly a school nurse."

"But you know people there?" I remembered something I'd heard in the teachers' lounge the day Amelia was found dead. "Your boyfriend Joey works there, doesn't he?"

"Yes."

"Is he a doctor?"

"He works in the ER."

Behind her, Jerry put a finger on his nose. Bingo.

"Helps out with supplies and things?" I asked as casually as I could.

"He does all kinds of work there. He's really very smart."

"So if you needed something, or someone here needed something, he could get it for you?"

She gave me another wide eyed look. This look wasn't dull.

This look looked frightened. "Oh, no. That's not permitted."

"So if someone asked you to get them some cold medicine, let's say, you wouldn't ask Joey to pick up some extra samples?"

"He wouldn't do that."

"Not even as a favor for you?"

She gave me another frightened look and fidgeted with the papers on her desk. "If you don't have any more questions, I have lots of paperwork to fill out."

"Okay."

"I was at the high school when Amelia Lever died."

"Yes, you told me. I believe you."

"And she had a heart attack, that's all. I don't know why you're going around stirring things up."

"Thanks for your time."

Jerry and I squeezed ourselves out of the tiny room and walked down the hallway back toward the office.

"I believe you hit a nerve—if she has any," Jerry said.

"I believe I did. Come on, there are a few classrooms I want to check."

Thad Murphy had lent me his master key, but Mrs. Lever's former classroom was unlocked. The room was cluttered with flowers, stuffed animals, a fountain, a fish tank, and a cage containing two fat guinea pigs that whistled shrilly at the intrusion.

"Good job, watchpigs," Jerry said. He scratched their heads. "I wish my fifth grade classroom had looked like this. It's Disneyland."

Loops of little Christmas lights hung from the ceiling. Posters covered every inch of the walls. The students' homework was displayed on every bulletin board, their papers decorated with stars and stickers and stamps that said, "Excellent Work!" and "I Knew You Could Do It."

"What are we looking for?" he asked. "Besides rainbows and unicorns?"

"I'm not sure."

Jerry looked in the mini-fridge. "Here's some deadly yogurt and a caffeine free Pepsi."

"Mrs. Dorman's, I bet."

"Oh, hello," said a cheerful voice.

Jerry and I turned to see Norma Olsen enter with her arms full of bright yellow and orange artificial leaves and pumpkins. The fact that we had just been poking around in her refrigerator didn't seem to bother her.

"I'm so glad you stopped by," she said. "I found some more of Amelia's things way back in the storage closet."

"The room looks wonderful," I said. "I'm sure the kids enjoy it."

She put the leaves and pumpkins on the nearest desk. "I know they do. The only thing Amelia had on the wall was the periodic table of the elements. That's something they should know, but it's not very entertaining. I found these great leaves at the Bargain Hut. I want the room to be like a forest in the fall." She went to the closet at the back of the classroom. "Let me get those things for you. Did you need to see me about something?"

"No, we're just looking around. I'm trying to get a sense of what might have happened to Amelia."

"If you ask me, it was all the stress she put on herself. You can't be that unhappy and not have some medical issues. Here we are." She pulled a bag out of the closet. "I don't know how helpful these things will be, but I don't want cigarettes in my classroom."

I was hoping for a spectacular clue. All I got were two more packs of cigarettes, a lighter, a travel pack of Kleenex, and a crumpled piece of paper with the initials "B.F." written on it.

"'Best Friends,'" Jerry said. "She liked you better than you thought, Norma."

She didn't appreciate his joke. "I'm sure it means something else, something mean and spiteful."

"'Butt-Face,' perhaps?"

I thought we'd better go before Jerry got more creative. "Thanks, Norma. You never know what might be useful."

She turned her smile back on high beam. "You let me know if there's anything I can do."

When we were in the hallway, I said, "Let's check out the art room."

In the art room, I paused before a display of the students' work. They'd done a good job on the still life and on their drawings of faces. I could see some real talent here.

Jerry came and stood beside me. "If this private investigator job doesn't work out, you could become a teacher."

"No, thanks. That takes far more patience than I'll ever possess."

"These pictures look good, though. I can see the Maclin influence."

We opened all the cabinets and drawers. They were filled with all sizes of colored paper, tape, scissors, and bottles of glue. A cabinet with long narrow shelves held art prints.

Jerry opened a door at the back of the room. "What's this?"

"That's a kiln for pottery and clay projects."

"Pretty nifty. Hang on."

"What?"

"Come look at this."

Crumpled up in the trash can next to the kiln were some charred scraps of blue cloth. Jerry handed them to me and then pulled out what looked like the rim of a baseball cap. He turned to me, eyes wide. "*Rachel* hit me from behind and stole the cards?"

I hadn't thought of it before, but Rachel was a small, slim woman who could be mistaken for a teenager, especially if she hid her hair under a baseball cap. "That's what it looks like. And then she burned the evidence— most of it." I took the scraps and put them in my pocket.

Jerry closed the door to the kiln. "Anything in her desk?"

"The usual stuff, paper clips, rubber bands." I paused. On the desk was a framed photograph of Bronwen and Magwen. Stuck in the picture frame was a card that read Diabetes Clinic. Free Seminars. Get Advice From the Experts. "Jerry, take a look at this."

He took the card and examined it. "So maybe Rachel's diabetic."

"Or one of the girls is." I put the card back in the frame. I sat down on one of the tables and stared at the rows of still life pictures. "Let's suppose Rachel's the killer. She knows Amelia goes for a smoke at one thirty. She fills one of her insulin syringes with potassium she got from Brenda Mullins, who got it from her boyfriend, lord knows why."

"She's so daffy, Rachel could've told her any sort of story."

"Right. Rachel comes in behind Amelia and injects the potassium. Amelia falls, and while Jacey races to call Murphy, Rachel doesn't perform CPR. Amelia dies. Rachel must've known about the riddle." I thought of something Ronald Brown had told me. He'd overheard Amelia tell Rachel, "I know all about it." All about what? And Rachel had replied, "You're just saying that so you'll get the money." I thought they'd been talking about the art grant. Maybe they'd been talking about the riddle."

"But did Rachel have time to do this?"

"She says she went to the office with a student to deliver some art work. Then she stopped by the loading dock to speak with Jacey."

"Could she have had a needle with her?"

I tried to recall the day of the incident. "A little girl stopped by the art room. Rachel left with her. She was carrying a big stack of art work. I suppose she could've had the syringe in her pocket."

"You remember which little girl it was?"

"Her name was Jennifer, but that's not going to be much help. I've noticed there are a lot of Jennifers in this school."

"Yo! Miz Fairweather!" Ronald Brown beamed from the door. "What are you doing here? Looking for clues?"

"Yes, I am," I said. "What are you doing here this late?"

He shrugged. "I had to stay after school. Timothy

and me got into a fight." He stood aside so we could see Timothy, a thin weedy-looking boy who didn't look like the type to cause trouble. He peered at me like a little owl behind his thick round glasses.

"You were right, Ron. She's a babe."

Ronald elbowed him. "Dude. That's her husband standing right there."

"It's okay," Jerry said. "She is a babe."

"Ronald, maybe you can help me," I said. "You remember the other day when a student named Jennifer came by the art room, and Mrs. Sigmon left to help her carry some art work to the office? Do you know Jennifer?"

Ronald made a gagging sound. "Jennifer Elson, teacher's pet. She gets to do everything, and most times, she doesn't even have to have a hall pass."

Timothy sniggered. "She dropped that whole pile of pictures, though. Splat! I busted a gut watching."

"Where did this happen?" I asked.

"In the office. I was there because I left my homework at home."

"For the fiftieth time," Ronald said.

"Hey, it's homework, isn't it? Why can't it be at home?"

"Guys," I said. "Timothy, this is important. Was Mrs. Sigmon with Jennifer?"

"No, I didn't see her, just Jennifer, trying to win more brownie points. She thinks she's so smart."

If Rachel gave Jennifer all the pictures and told her to go on to the office by herself, then Rachel would have had more time—if she was responsible for Amelia's death. But this still didn't explain why Rachel would feel entitled to any of the Fenton fortune. Then again,

Misty May had explained that whoever showed up with the correct key would get the prize money.

"Thanks," I told the boys.

"Did we solve the crime?" Ronald asked.

"Not yet."

Timothy's eyes gleamed. "Got any suspects? I hope it's Mrs. Sigmon."

"I hope it's her snotty daughters, Bran and Mud," Ronald said. "I wasn't invited to Bran's birthday party because my dad's not rich enough. Timothy's dad owns a bank, so he got to go."

"Yeah, and she had all these Bufo cards, even some of the new ones, too. I don't know how she got them before anybody else did."

"They were lousy, though. You said so."

"That's 'cause they're so lame. I'm collecting Wrath cards now. I've got Thief of Wrath, Cloud of Wrath, Castle of Wrath. That's the hardest one to find."

Thad Murphy's voice sounded over the PA system. "Ronald Brown and Timothy Ashboro, your rides are waiting."

"Whoops, gotta go," Ronald said.

He and Timothy raced up the hall.

"Wrath cards," Jerry said. "Wonder if Austin and Denisha know about that."

"Well, we know how Bronwen got new Bufo cards before anyone else."

My cell phone rang and I answered. Tori's little voice said, "Madeline? I hope I'm not disturbing you."

"Not at all, Tori."

"Well, I need some help if you have time. In all the excitement, we forgot Cousin Barnaby. He's still in the dining room, and he's not very good company. Could Jerry come put him back where he belongs?"

"We'll be right there."

I hung up. "We forgot and left Cousin Barnaby in the dining room, and Tori's tired of him staring at her."

"We can fix that."

TORI BEAMED at us. "Thanks for coming so soon. I hope I didn't interrupt anything important."

"Not at all," I said. "I'm a little stuck right now anyway." And I knew Tori was trying to find ways to have our company.

In the dining room, Cousin Barnaby glared from his portrait. Tori patted the frame. "I think I've memorized every little bit of this picture, and it wasn't even the one we needed."

Jerry picked up the portrait. "Where does he go?"

"Down in the main hall."

We walked down the long dim corridor to the right place. Jerry angled the portrait back on its hook, and we stood back to admire the old codger.

"If you get lonely for him, I can always carry him back," Jerry said.

Tori laughed. "That won't be for a long while. He'd be nice looking if he'd smile. He has nice eyes and the cutest little notch in his ear."

"What?" I said.

"It's a little hard to see, but his ear has a "V" shaped notch."

"Jerry, would you please take Cousin Barnaby down?"

"Okay," he said, puzzled.

He took the picture off the wall and propped it

where it had the best light. We'd been so involved in the riddle, the sparrow, the river, and all those clues, I hadn't noticed the finer features of Cousin Barnaby. Sure enough, his ear had a "V" shaped notch, exactly like the notch in Rachel Sigmon's ear. Then I thought of something else. Could the "B.F." Amelia had written refer to Barnaby Fenton?

"Tori, do you have any sort of family record book?"

"A record book?"

"A family tree, a genealogy, a history?"

"There's a family Bible that belonged to Elijah."

"Great! May I see it?"

"It's somewhere around here."

After about fifteen minutes of searching through the books in another dark room, we unearthed a huge Bible. We took it to Tori's den and put it on the table on top of her latest scrapbook. Jerry brought a lamp closer so we could read the small handwriting. The list of Fentons included all the Fentons we'd found in the hallway and in the attic, and of course, Elijah, Ellis, and Eulalie, along with Ellis' wife, Henrietta, and their son, Nathan, and Eulalie's husband, Thomas Satterfield, and their son, Aaron. But there was also a Clara Fenton and a Rachel Fenton. Both of these names had lines drawn through them.

"Whoops," Jerry said. "Looks like someone's illegitimate."

"But I've never heard of Clara and Rachel Fenton," Tori said.

I finally had a connection. "This might explain why Rachel thinks she's entitled to the money. Maybe Clara's her mother, and Elijah's her dad."

"A dad who didn't want to claim her."

"Tori, do you know anything about this?" I asked.

"No. I'm amazed."

"We need to find someone who would know all the details." Jerry and I thought of someone at the same moment.

"Nell," we said.

I took out my cell phone and punched in Nell's number.

"Oh, yeah," she said when I told her what we needed to know. "Hang on a second. Dad's here. I'll ask him." I waited a few minutes until she came back on the line. "There's a Clara Bennett Dad said Elijah used to see. Maybe she's the same one."

"I need to talk to Clara. Is that possible?"

"She's in the Century City Retirement Village."

"Thanks."

"You're thinking Rachel Sigmon's the same Rachel?"

"What was her maiden name?"

"She was a Mills—oh, and Dad said to tell you that if you have any theories, you'd better share them with him at your earliest convenience. That wasn't exactly how he said it. I cleaned up that last part."

"Thanks, Nell. Tell him he's at the top of my to do list."

She gave a snort and hung up.

I closed my phone. "We're taking a side trip to Century City Retirement Village. Tori, want to come along?"

"Oh, no, thank you," she said. "But you have to let me know how this all turns out."

CENTURY CITY Retirement Village was a large complex of Colonial style apartments. The receptionist directed us to the skilled care unit, another series of brick buildings. Clara Bennett Mills was in room sixty-two, sitting in a wheel chair. She was a small woman, bent over and feeble, with pale blue eyes.

"I'm not sure who you are," she said to me, "but that handsome young man with you has to be Edward."

Jerry pulled up a chair and sat next to her. He took her hand in his. "How are you feeling today, Miss Clara?"

"Oh, 'bout the same," she said. "My health's not good, you know."

"I'm sorry to hear that."

"Is Margaret with you?"

"Not today. Rachel might stop by later, though."

"Huh! She never stops by."

"Your daughter Rachel doesn't visit you?" I asked.

"After all I've done for her, too. She's ungrateful. Always has been."

"What about her father? What about Elijah Fenton?" Clara's face drew in with anger. "Fenton! Didn't leave me a dime! Told her she was going to have to wait for it. He left me for that Lever woman and said he'd leave her a fortune!"

"Elijah left you for Amelia Lever."

"Didn't I just say that? Edward, tell her what I just said."

"Elijah left her for Amelia Lever," Jerry said.

"Didn't marry her, neither."

I sat down on the bed for a closer look at Clara Mills. She couldn't have been more than sixty, but her face was lined and her eyes weren't clear. I couldn't see any resemblance to Rachel, but Clara obviously had had a hard life. "Does Rachel know Elijah was her father?"

"I told her a hundred times she could get in good with the family. She was a Fenton, too. But he disowned us. Said we'd get nothing. Told his family we were making up lies."

"So you were never actually married to him?"

"Had to keep things quiet. Back then, people didn't understand. Nowadays you can parade around and have as many children as you like out of wedlock. Nobody says a thing. But Rachel's entitled to her share."

"You told Rachel that."

"When we were speaking to each other, yes." She looked around. "Where is she? Did she come with you?"

"No," I said. "Did Elijah discuss his will with you?"

She gripped the arm of the wheelchair. "No! And how do you think I found out I was getting nothing? After I had Rachel, he didn't want to have anything to do with me, or with her. I came to his house one day to tell him to give me some money for his daughter— he was still in the big house and not in that trailer— and I was in his study and found some papers on his desk that said he was going to leave all his money to whoever outlived him. I told Rachel that was the craziest thing I ever heard of. Why not divide the money among the real family members like any sensible person would do? Oh, no, not Elijah. He had to be clever. He had to make everyone jump around."

"Mrs. Mills, are you sure that's what you saw? There wasn't a riddle someone had to solve? Or mention of bat houses?"

She shook her head. "He had three names written down. Aaron and Nathan I could understand, but that Lever woman? She wasn't even family! My name should've been on that list, and Rachel's!" She paused to catch her breath. Her whole body shook. "My health's not good."

I needed to change the subject before Clara had a serious episode. A small bulletin board on the wall was covered with photographs of smiling children. "Are these your children?"

"And grandchildren."

"You married, then."

"That's him right there, Sebastian Mills, a good man, rest his soul. That's Amanda and Susan and Paul and Edward and their children. I can't think of all their names just now."

There were no pictures of Rachel, or Bronwen and Magwen. "You have a lovely family."

She gave Jerry another look. "You're not Edward."

"No, ma'am," he said, "but I'm a good friend of Edward's."

"Well, you tell him to come see me and bring those little boys of his."

"I certainly will." I saw him eying the large gold pocket watch on her dresser. "That's a beautiful watch, Mrs. Mills. May I have a closer look?"

"Yes, of course," she said.

I gave him a warning glance—was he planning to take it right out from under this poor old woman?— but he grinned wryly as he showed me the large fancy "M" engraved on the lid. "Very nice."

"My husband had excellent taste."

A pleasant-looking woman in a flowered smock came in the room. She was pushing a cart filled with medical supplies. "Glad to see you have visitors, Mrs. Mills. It's almost time for your meds, though."

Clara sighed. "My health's not good, you know. But I'm still living. That's more than can be said for Elijah Fenton or Amelia Lever."

I looked at the little trays on the cart, each one labeled and numbered. "If you don't mind me asking, what sort of health problems do you have?"

"Blood pressure's high, and I've got sugar."

"She means diabetes," the nurse said. "I've got your shot right here, Mrs. Mills."

Clara smiled. "This gal knows what she's doing."

"We're going to take care of you," the nurse said. "You'll feel better, I promise."

I saw something I recognized on the nurse's cart. The syringe had a plastic cap on the end to cover the needle, a cap exactly like the one I'd found in the grass beside the loading dock. I gave Jerry a glance and he nodded. He'd seen it, too.

Jerry patted Clara's hand. "We have to go. Thank you, Mrs. Mills. You've been very helpful."

She waved us good-by. "You're welcome."

"Extremely helpful," I said as we walked back down the hall.

"Except for having a last name that begins with 'M.'"

"You almost gave me a stroke in there. Would you have taken that watch if it had an 'S' on it?"

"Well, it didn't."

I caught his arm and stopped him. "Jerry."

"Take it easy," he said. "I wouldn't have stolen it. Maybe borrowed it for a little while."

"Why don't you just tell Flossie Mae and Sylvie the truth? Let me deal with Jackson Dooly and his relatives."

"I could always say the watch has an 'M' for Marie and Marge."

I stared to sputter, and he started to laugh. "Mac, relax! Bilby said the watch would be ready tomorrow. I've still got time."

"All right. I'll go talk to Rachel. Clara must have seen an earlier version of Elijah's will. If Clara told Rachel the money went to the last man standing, then Rachel's trying to bump off everyone who's in her way. She got rid of Amelia, and I think she made an attempt to get to Aaron."

"But the game's over," Jerry said. "Nathan solved the riddle. There's no way she could claim it now even if she really is Elijah's daughter."

"I'm willing to bet she didn't know about the riddle. Ronald Brown overheard Amelia tell her, 'Oh, you don't know anything about it.' The game changed."

"But if she stole the Bufo cards, she must have known something about the riddle."

"Maybe she knew just enough." I checked my watch. "It's almost six. I think the girls have their dance recital tonight. Rachel wouldn't miss that. She'll be at the theater. We're going by Nathan's first to make sure he's all right. I might need you to stay with him, just in case."

"No problem."

NATHAN WAS HOME and happily involved with the paperwork for his camp.

"Come in, come in! I'm almost done with all this!"

"Thought you might like some help," Jerry said.

"Oh, yeah, sure. Just clear a path and start straightening stacks. I've got all the sponsors over here and all the registration stuff over there." He took a deep breath.

"I can't thank you enough for helping me, Madeline. I know I wasn't very agreeable at times, and I kept things from you I should've mentioned at the very beginning, but Amelia had warned me about someone trying to get the money—and well, I almost ruined everything."

"But you didn't," I said.

"And poor Tori all alone in that big house. I really want to do something for her to make up for all the misunderstanding."

"I'm sure she'd appreciate that." I thought of Fiona's concerns about Nathan and Tori. "Have you called Fiona?"

"I did. She was the first one I called. She's very happy for me." He blushed. "I may even pop the question now that I have something to offer her."

Fiona's concerns were now resolved. "That's great." I gave Jerry a quick kiss. "I'll see you later. Nathan, I've got an errand to run and I'll be back."

THE PARKING LOT, theater lobby, and backstage areas at Celosia's community theater building were jammed with parents, grandparents, and assorted relatives all accompanying little girls and boys in fluorescent costumes. I wasn't sure I'd be able to find Rachel or her daughters in such a crowd.

"Hi, Madeline!"

I was surprised to see Fiona making her way upstream through the rows of children. "I didn't expect to see you here."

"I have three nieces in this recital. I'd better be here. Isn't that terrific news about Nathan? He called and told me all about it."

"I hope you were able to talk about other things, too."

The lights were dim backstage, but I believe Fiona blushed. "Yes, we had a good discussion. He did care for Tori, but now they're just friends."

"Good," I said. "Now maybe you can help me. I'm looking for Rachel Sigmon or one of her girls."

Fiona turned and pointed behind her. "They should be in one of the big rooms downstairs. I just helped my brother get all his girls situated. You'll need to hurry. The dance instructors want all adults out in five minutes."

"Thanks."

"Madeline, I know Nathan appreciates all your help, and so do I."

"You're welcome. I'm glad we figured out the riddle before the deadline." Then I thought of something Fiona had figured out. "Fiona, Nathan said you thought the Bufo cards might have been part of the game. What made you think that?"

She shrugged. "I don't know. I just thought packs might mean packs of cards. But the riddle said, 'Trust animals that live in packs,' and cartoon toads certainly aren't living, so I dismissed the notion as too silly. I'm glad you had more imagination than I."

"Did you by any chance discuss the riddle with Rachel?"

"No, of course not. Now, I knew her girls wanted some Bufo cards, and I did tell her Nathan had gotten all these packs of cards in the mail, and maybe she could have those. But then he decided to keep them for his campers."

"When did you tell her this?"

"Oh, some time ago."

"Before last Tuesday?" That was the day Georgia's had been robbed.

"Yes, I'm sure it was before then."

Rachel hadn't dismissed the notion as silly. Rachel had decided she needed as many packs of Bufo cards as she could get. I needed to find her. I made my way downstairs to the dance studios through the mothers, daughters, grandmothers, and aunts. Bronwen and Magwen sat in their dressing area playing games on their cell phones. Bronwen's dress was yellow with rows and rows of shiny ribbon. Magwen was in a pink lace pleated number that made her look like a cupcake. I didn't see Rachel.

"Hi, girls. Where's your mother?"

Bronwen glanced up. "She forgot one of my costumes, so she went home to get it."

My nerves went on high alert. Was Rachel likely to forget one of her daughter's important dance costumes? "When did she leave?"

"Just a few minutes ago. I told her she didn't need to hurry because my first number's way down on the program."

I stepped outside and called Jerry. Two rings, three rings— where the hell was he? I was getting anxious. I imagined Rachel armed with deadly syringes, sneaking into Nathan's house. When Jerry finally answered, I said, "Are you okay? You need to get out of the house. Rachel's not here."

"We're not here, either," he said. "I convinced Nathan we needed to go out for pizza. We're at Mario's."

My knees almost buckled with relief. "Good move.

She may not go after Nathan, but I don't want to take any chances."

"We'll stay put until I hear from you."

"Thanks."

"You're not going to do anything stupid, are you?"

"No, I'm going to wait for her here."

As soon as I closed my phone, I knew I wasn't going to wait. Rachel wouldn't miss her daughters' dance recital. She might be planning some sort of trap for Nathan. If she set her trap and came back to the theater, she'd have her alibi. I'd better check. And I decided I needed a witness.

CHIEF BRENNER answered on the second ring. "Yes, Ms. Maclin?"

"I'd like you to meet me at Nathan Fenton's," I said. "I have reason to believe he may be in danger."

I'm sure the fact that I'd solved two murders in his town gave me a little credibility. "Anything in particular I should know?" he asked.

"I'm hoping Rachel Sigmon will give herself away."

NATHAN HAD LEFT the lights on. The back door was unlocked. This didn't seem reasonable, even in Celosia. I entered as quietly as I could. Someone was in the living room.

"Hello, Rachel," I said.

She didn't whirl around in surprise. She calmly turned and smiled at me. "Hello, Madeline."

"What are you doing here?"

She took a key out of her shoulder bag. "Fiona lent me her key. She left her wallet here at Nathan's. I told her I'd stop by and pick it up for her. She said she'd watch the girls."

"That's very nice of you."

"What are you doing here, Madeline?"

"I wanted to see how Nathan's plans for his camp are coming along. Is he home?"

"I don't know where he is. He must've stepped out for a minute." She moved toward the front door. "I really need to get back to the theater."

"Where's the wallet?" I asked.

"What?"

"Fiona's wallet that you came for. Where is it?"

She shrugged. "I guess she didn't leave it, after all. You know how flighty she is."

"Flighty" was not a word I'd use to describe Fiona. "I don't think she gave you her key."

She put her hand on the doorknob. "What do you mean by that?"

"I think in all the confusion backstage, you borrowed it."

"Really?"

"I'm finding it hard to believe you'd leave your daughters on this important night to come over to Nathan Fenton's house. I don't think Fiona would need her wallet that badly, either. She could pick it up after the recital."

Rachel turned and faced me. "Are you accusing me of something?"

"I remember that first day in the teacher's lounge when you told Josh Kellogg the art grant was not something you'd kill for. I think I know what you'd kill for. You'd kill for the chance at Elijah Fenton's money."

"And what exactly do you mean by that?"

"You're Elijah Fenton's illegitimate daughter."

She gave a little start of surprise. "How do you know that?"

"The notch in your ear. It's a Fenton thing."

She almost raised her hand to her ear but caught herself. She raised her chin instead. "Well, what if I am? There's nothing wrong about it."

"Except your mother told you that you have some claim to the fortune. But she didn't have all the information."

"When did you talk to my mother? Why would you talk to her? She's been in a rest home for years. She doesn't even know who I am half the time."

"Your mother saw an earlier version of Elijah's game plan. She saw three names on a list: Aaron Satterfield, Nathan Fenton, and Amelia Lever. She thought they had to be out of the way before she or you could have a chance, and that's what she told you. You already hated Amelia for terrifying Bronwen."

"I had every right to move my daughter to another school. Amelia Lever was a monster. She should never have been allowed in a classroom." Her eyes narrowed. "What are you trying to say?"

"You knew she went out on the loading dock at one thirty every afternoon to smoke and that no one else would be out there except Jacey. You told Jennifer to stop by the art room at one thirty, but you didn't go with her to the office. You sent her on while you went to the loading dock, came up behind Amelia, and injected her, knowing too much potassium would cause a heart attack. Actually, that was a pretty gutsy move, because Jacey could have seen you, but you were behind Amelia, and she was a much larger woman. And

Jacey wasn't her friend, so Jacey was probably standing at the other end of the dock. Amelia gasped and fell down. Then you sent Jacey for help while you pretended to administer CPR." I took out the little plastic cap. "I found this out by the loading dock. I wasn't sure what it was at first, but it's a cap you put on the end of a syringe. I think you inherited diabetes from your mother and you're pretty handy with a needle."

Rachel didn't say anything. She watched me with an intense stare, her body tense as if poised for flight.

"You also robbed Georgia's Books," I said.

"Are you crazy?"

"Jerry and I found the remains of your blue jacket and cap in the kiln, and there were loads of gold wrappers in your trash can. You tried to put the blame on Bobby Berkely, but you didn't know he was still in reform school. By the way, why didn't you just buy the cards yourself? No one would have thought anything of it."

"You don't know what you're talking about."

"You knew about the riddle. And when Fiona mentioned that Nathan had received Bufo cards in the mail, you thought there might be something in this. Or maybe Amelia taunted you. She told you you didn't know anything about it. That 'it' was the riddle, right?"

"I bought cards for Bronwen's birthday party."

I took the pieces of jacket and cap from my pocket. "You want to explain this away, too?" I saw her swallow hard. "I also think you made an attempt on Aaron, but his security system kept you out. Then Nathan Fenton solved the riddle. So now you have to get rid of Nathan. It's easy to believe Amelia Lever had a heart attack, but a young man in his thirties like Nathan? Too much coincidence."

Her expression hardened. "I am entitled to that money."

"No, I'm afraid not."

"My mother told me!"

"Your mother didn't have all the facts."

She clenched her fist. "It isn't fair. My husband left me to raise two girls all by myself. If Aaron and Nathan are dead, then I'm next in line for the Fenton money."

"No, you're not, and Nathan isn't going to be dead."

"Yes, I think he is. How do you plan to stop me?" She reached into her shoulder bag and brought out a syringe. "This was supposed to be for Nathan," she said. "But I think you'll do."

"No one's going to believe I died of a heart attack, too."

"Oh, they might." She kept herself between me and the front door. "After all, you're trying to keep your agency going in a small town. That can be stressful."

"Not that stressful. How did you get potassium?"

"Brenda's so stupid, she's easy to blackmail. I told her if she didn't get some for me, I'd have that boyfriend of her fired for stealing medical supplies. She actually believed I had that kind of clout."

Between the stacks of papers and the trash, there wasn't a lot of room to back away. "But Brenda stole it for you."

"She did a good job, considering she's so thick. I didn't need much." She advanced. "I'm glad Nathan's not much of a housekeeper. You really don't have anywhere to run except past me, and as you said, I'm pretty handy with a needle."

The way to the front door was blocked by the stacks of paper and Rachel. I had asked Brenner to come to Nathan's, but where was he? Could I jump over the counter and run for the back door? There wasn't enough room. What could I use as a weapon? I felt along the counter behind me. More papers, dried pizza, Bufo cards—Bufo cards! Well, maybe Rachel would like to play a game of Fifty-Two Pickup.

I bent the pack back as hard as I could, swung my hand around, and released the flapping spray of cards into Rachel's face. As she batted them away, I grabbed her wrist and held on as she tried to pull away. I slung her as hard as I could against the wall, but she fought back, jabbing the needle at my face. We slipped and fell in the piles of paper. I beat her hand on the floor until she finally let go of the syringe. As she scrabbled for it, I jumped up and stomped on it as hard as I could. Rachel grabbed my ankle, and I fell, but I fell back on top of her. She gave a "Whoof!" and lay still. At that moment, Brenner ran in from the back, and the front door slammed open and Jerry and Nathan ran in.

"You'll be happy to know I heard every word," Brenner said.

"I knew it," Jerry said to me. "I knew you'd be here." To Nathan, he said, "What did I tell you? I knew she couldn't stay put." He helped me up. "Are you okay?"

I nodded. I caught my breath. "Nathan, meet your ex-cousin, Rachel."

SEVEN

IT TOOK A LONG TIME to settle everything, but by the end of the evening, Rachel had been formally charged with the murder of Amelia Lever. Her husband was called to come take care of his daughters. Jerry and I got home very early in the morning and tried to get some sleep. Finally, around eight, we got up, and Jerry made some coffee and toast.

"Oh, in all the excitement, I forgot to tell you," he said as he brought a plate of toast to the table. "Since my old friends aren't very dependable, I thought it might be time to make some new friends. While Nathan and I were having pizza, he invited me to help with his camp."

"What? You mean, help him run it?"

He passed me the butter. "Yeah."

"Do you know anything about running a children's camp?"

"No, but it sounds like fun."

Of course, I thought, knowing how Austin and Denisha loved having Jerry involved with their projects, and how pleased Tori had been by Jerry's magic tricks. A camp full of children would be the perfect place for him.

I buttered my toast and slid the butter dish back to him. "I think that's great. You'll be surrounded by kids."

"And Nathan will pay me. In fact, when I explained my situation, he advanced me a thousand dollars."

"That's the kind of new friend I like."

"That's two jobs I have now. You're falling behind."

"Not for long," I said. "I've got one more picture to finish, and I'm going to paint all day."

"And I'm heading to Parkland for one more try at a watch."

I decided not to comment on this. I was drinking the last of my coffee when I got a call from Marshall Lever.

"Madeline, we heard the news about Rachel Sigmon. I'm not sure what to say."

"Are you and your brother all right?"

"Yes, thanks to you." There was a moment of silence, and then he said, "I don't know if this will be of any use to you now, but we know where that boy is, the one in the photograph, Ronald McIntire. Twelve thirty-eight Kent Place East in Madison. We found the address in some of Mother's things."

"Thank you."

"We always resented the fact she sent him money. We knew that somehow he was the kind of son she always wanted. It's time to let go of that. We have new lives now."

"Good luck to both of you."

"Well, what do you know," I said as I closed my phone. "Marshall and Kevin gave me Rusty's address. He's not that far away, and I'm really curious about him. Let's pay him a call."

"Got to find a watch," Jerry said.

"Rusty lives in Madison. We'll look for your watch on the way back."

MADISON WAS LOCATED on the other side of Parkland. Twelve thirty-eight Kent Place East was the Madison County Hospital.

"Uh, oh," I said. "We may be too late."

We went to the main desk and asked to see Ronald McIntire.

The receptionist smiled. "Doctor McIntire is on the second floor. His office is two ten."

I looked at Jerry. "Doctor McIntire."

"I'll see if he's available."

After a few minutes, the receptionist told us to go on up to the second floor where we found Doctor McIntire's office. The man who came out to greet us still had the dark eyes and earnest expression I'd seen in his childhood photo. He had on a white lab coat and a stethoscope around his neck. His nametag said, "Dr. Ronald S. McIntire, M.D."

"I'm Ron McIntire," he said. "How can I help you?"

We shook hands. "I'm Madeline Maclin Fairweather and this is my husband, Jerry Fairweather. We'd like to know if you ever had a teacher named Amelia Lever."

He brightened. "Has she finally changed her mind?"

"Changed her mind?"

"About contacting me."

"I'm sorry to tell you she died of a heart attack a few days ago."

"Oh, no." His bright expression faded. He swallowed hard. "Now I'll never be able to thank her."

Jerry and I must have looked confused. "I should explain," McIntire said. He led us to a corner of the waiting area, and we sat down. "About ten years ago, I received a letter from Mrs. Lever saying she was going to finance my education, but if I told anyone, I'd forfeit the money. I guess she was afraid my parents would try to take it from me. I'd left home by then and had no idea what to do. Every month, she'd send me some money. That money saved me. So many times I wanted to write or call her, but she refused any contact. Something about her sons not understanding."

"So she financed your medical career?"

He gestured around the room. "Everything you see here was made possible by Mrs. Lever's generosity, my career, this hospital, everything. Were you friends of hers?"

"We didn't get to know her. You've solved one part of the mystery. How did she know where to find you ten years ago?"

"I wrote her a letter, telling her how much I missed her and how she'd helped me so much."

"And that's when she sent you the money."

"Yes, with strict instructions not to tell anyone or write back. It's been very hard, because I've been so grateful. Now she'll never know. At least I can thank you for coming to tell me. Wish I could do more."

Before we left, McIntire gave us a short tour of the hospital. I couldn't help but think of all the good Amelia Lever had done that no one ever knew about, not even her sons. Well, I'd be sure to tell them. It was time they had different memories of their mother.

THERE WAS NO gold watch for Jerry in Parkland. Bilby's source had backed out on him, and there wasn't anything the pawn-broker could do.

"I can't believe this," Jerry said as we drove home.

"Mac, I'm sorry. If the *Celosia News* gives you trouble, I'll make it up to you somehow."

"Don't worry about it. You see how all these schemes backfire, don't you? Doesn't that tell you something, like get out while you still can, while you still have all your limbs attached?"

"Yeah, well, maybe."

"You're lucky Bert didn't punch you. You can't expect a gold watch to fall out of the sky."

"Guess not."

WHEN WE GOT TO the house, Austin and Denisha were sitting on the front porch. Ronald Brown was with them.

"Ronald wanted to hear all about the needle fight," Austin said.

"There wasn't really a needle fight," I said.

Ronald's eyes were gleaming. "I heard you and Mrs. Sigmon went three rounds. Knew you could take her."

"Thanks, Ronald. Jerry, you want to see if Austin and Denisha can help you make some brownies?"

Austin leaped up. "Whoo-eee, brownies!"

He and Denisha followed Jerry into the house. I sat down on the porch steps with Ronald.

"It's like this, Ronald. Mrs. Sigmon thought she was entitled to some money, but she wasn't. It made her a little crazy, and she did some foolish things."

"She killed Mrs. Lever?"

"Yes."

He made a face. "Ms. Olsen's no good. I wish Mrs. Lever was still here."

"You can do something to make sure no one forgets her."

Ronald squinted up at me.

"You can become something. Something important. And when people ask you how you did it, you say, 'Mrs. Amelia Lever taught me.'" I took out Ronald McIntire's picture. "See this kid? His name's Ronald, too. About twenty years ago, Mrs. Lever had him in her class, and today, he's a doctor. He couldn't have done it without her help. She believed in him, and she believed in you, too."

"This kid became a doctor?"

"Even though he had a rotten family."

"Maybe she just liked kids named Ronald."

"Whatever the reason, that's one thing you can do to keep her memory alive."

He gave me a curious look, and I realized he'd probably never been entrusted with this kind of responsibility. He stood a little straighter. "I can do that?"

"Yes."

"It's sorta like getting Bufo's Power Stone, isn't it? The thing that makes everything else all right."

The thing that makes everything else all right. "It's exactly like that."

He thought a few more minutes. "Okay. I'll do it."

We shook hands. "Thank you, Ronald."

"I might not become a doctor, though."

"You can be whatever you like."

He corrected me. "Something important."

THE KIDS MADE a huge mess making brownies, but everyone enjoyed the results. Ronald talked Austin and Denisha into getting Wrath cards, so they decided to ride their bikes to town to buy some. Ordinarily, Jerry would've gone with them, but he was still pondering what to do about Flossie Mae and Sylvie.

"Just tell them the truth," I said. I sat down in one of the porch rocking chairs while Jerry sat on the railing.

"The truth. What an alien concept."

"Unless you want Jackson Dooley to rearrange your face."

He sighed. "It's not so much that as disappointing Flossie Mae and Sylvie."

"You should have thought about that before."

"I know. It's tough being thoughtful."

I got up. "Well, you have another whole day to think about it. I'm going to paint."

BY THE END of the day, I had gotten a lot of work done and was feeling more and more confident I'd be ready by Monday. Jerry still hadn't decided what to do about Flossie Mae and Sylvie. Sunday morning, he said, "Want to ride into town and get a copy of the *Herald?* I'm curious to see what Valerie wrote about you."

We rode down to the post office and bought a copy of the paper from the machine. As Jerry drove back home, I read the article aloud.

"'New Artist Investigates New Career.' Not a bad headline. 'Upcoming artist Madeline Maclin Fairweather has her sights set on two careers: painting and detecting. As owner of Maclin Investigations, she has successfully solved two murders in the neighboring town of Celosia.'"

"Make that three," Jerry said.

"'She is also one of the new artists to be featured in the Weyland Gallery's New Artist Show this weekend. Fairweather says her style is based on but not limited to Impressionism. She also enjoys representative landscapes and portraits. One of her portraits hangs in the lobby of the Baker Auditorium in Celosia. Fairweather moved from Parkland to Celosia to set up her own detective agency. She soon established herself as a reputable investigator. She had done a lot of painting while in college, and she discovered that she wanted to continue her artwork. When asked how she plans to balance the two very different careers, Fairweather replied, 'I can always make time for the things that are important to me.'" I folded the paper. "She goes on to say when the exhibit will be open and all that. I have to say it's a good article, short and to the point."

"Nice picture, too."

I took another look at the photo of me sitting in the booth at Deely's. Valerie was right. The light was good. I looked relaxed and well, competent. "I'd hire me. To paint or detect. Or both."

"And you're ready for the show?"

"A few finishing touches, and yes, I'll be ready." My cell phone rang, and I checked the caller ID. It was Tori. "Hold that thought," I said. "Hello, Tori."

"Madeline, I found the ties for Jerry. Do you think you'd have time to come by today?"

"Yes, of course."

"Can you come for lunch?"

"We'll be there." I closed the phone. "Tori's found some ties for you. That should cheer you up."

"Yes, it will," he said.

THE TIES WERE BEAUTIFUL silk ties in lovely subtle patterns, a far cry from Jerry's usual flying pigs and light bulbs. Tori carefully took each one out of the box. I could tell she wanted to prolong our visit. Over lunch, I answered all her questions about Rachel. She was relieved that Nathan was all right.

"And the little girls are with their father?"

"Yes, they'll be all right."

"You were so lucky she didn't hurt you, Madeline."

"She's tough," Jerry said. "She can handle anything. And so can you, Tori."

Tori nodded. "You know, I'm almost beginning to believe that. Do you know what I did? I called Aaron."

"You called him? What did he say?"

"I told him I was very sorry to hear about his partner. I said I wished he'd been honest with me, but I understood why he couldn't be. He was worried about what people here would think." Her smile trembled. "He said he was so sorry. He was crying a little. I told him it was okay. He's coming to visit me. We're going to see about getting a divorce and getting on with our lives. But I told him I'd like to be friends, if we could, and he said he'd like that, too."

"That's wonderful," I said. "So you don't blame yourself any more?"

She was practically beaming. "No, not at all. Oh, I almost forgot." She hopped up from the table and dug another box out of a dark corner of the dining room. "You might like to have this, too, Jerry. It belonged to Cousin Ivor Satterfield."

Jerry opened the box. He stared for a moment and then took out a gold pocket watch. Then he grinned and turned the watch so that I could see the "S" engraved on the lid.

"It has an 'S' for Satterfield," Tori said, "but I didn't think you'd mind."

I knew Jerry was thinking "S" for "Snyder." "Thanks, Tori. I don't mind at all. I can certainly use this."

"You lucky dog," I said sotto voce.

Tori turned to me. "Oh, and Madeline." She took a quick shaky little breath. "I-I've decided to come to the ballet, if you're going, if you're not too busy."

"Of course. That's great."

"I think I'll be okay."

"I know you will. Let me call and see if we can get tickets."

"Jerry, will you come, too?"

He smoothed the watch. "For you, Tori, anything."

She watched as I called the ballet company. "I do hope I don't lose my nerve."

Fortunately, the ballet was not sold out. I ordered three tickets and closed my phone. "Okay, we're all set. Sleeping Beauty next Saturday at eight."

She grasped my hand with her fragile little fingers. "Oh, Madeline," she said, her large eyes shining with tears. "Thank you so much. I know it will be beautiful."

I knew she was remembering her one night of triumph, the one night when everything was all right with her world, the one night when she was a star.

"You're welcome, Tori."

"Really, how can I ever thank you?"

Jerry grinned as he held up the gold watch. "Believe me, Tori. This makes everything more than even."

JERRY ADMIRED his new watch and chuckled all the way home.

"No one deserves to be that lucky," I said.

"It's a sign."

"No, it isn't."

"A special kind of sign."

I sighed. I could see "Jerry Fairweather, Super Psychic" in neon flashing from our front window. "No."

"A sign that says, 'Justice Rules the Swamp.'"

"It's not justice. It's incredible coincidence."

Jerry grinned. "How about a sign that says, 'You get only one incredible coincidence in your life. Get out while you can.'"

"Don't tease me."

"I mean it. I'm done."

I wasn't sure how long this would last. "Well, if you're serious, that's great."

"I can't have Hortensia picking up my bad habits."

Dear me, I thought. If he gives up his cons and schemes, he's going to have more time to think about babies. I have to find another way to divert his attention.

He turned on the CD player. "This calls for a little Hoffmann."

A joyful duet filled the car. "What are they saying?"

"Hoffmann and Antonia are singing, 'Happy married couple, the future is ours! Ours!'"

"Antonia. She dies, doesn't she?"

"It's opera, Mac. You can't have everything."

"I'm just saying they didn't have much of a future. Doesn't the portrait of her mother come to life and cause her to sing herself to death?"

"Yes, but that's not likely to happen to you. And speaking of portraits, are you going to be ready for the show?"

"I have the rest of today and tonight to work. A little more work on Austin and Denisha's picture, and I'll be ready."

"I knew you could do it."

"Thanks."

"Just like I knew you could solve this case."

I thought of sensitive little Tori hiding herself away because she didn't have all the facts. I thought of the Lever brothers and how they never realized the good their mother could do. I thought of poor spurned Clara trying to convince her daughter she was entitled to a fortune. With this little bit of misinformation, she'd caused Rachel nothing but frustration and grief and the rest of her life in prison. By comparison, what my mother had done to me by hauling me to pageants was just a mild inconvenience. I found myself hoping she'd come to the exhibit, even looking forward to it.

Jerry turned up the volume. "Listen to this part. 'To love let us be true! May its eternal chains keep our hearts victorious over time itself.' Not sure I like the eternal chains. That's a tall order, isn't it?"

"I think we can do it."

"Happy married couple, the future is ours, ours?"

We had almost reached our driveway, but I pulled over next to the field full of wildflowers, the field that led up to our house, the one place in the world I knew I really wanted to be. Maybe this was how *Tales of Hoffmann* fit into our lives. "Happy married couple, the future is ours, ours"? I gave Jerry a long, lingering, and relieved kiss.

"Yes," I said. "Yes."

* * * * *

REQUEST YOUR FREE BOOKS!

2 FREE NOVELS
PLUS 2 FREE GIFTS!

WORLDWIDE LIBRARY®
MYSTERY

Your Partner in Crime